THE DEVIL AND THE VISCOUNT

Gentlemen of Pleasure, Book 1

Mary Lancaster

© Copyright 2022 by Mary Lancaster
Text by Mary Lancaster
Cover by Dar Albert

Dragonblade Publishing, Inc. is an imprint of Kathryn Le Veque Novels, Inc.
P.O. Box 23
Moreno Valley, CA 92556
ceo@dragonbladepublishing.com

Produced in the United States of America

First Edition April 2022
Trade Paperback Edition

Reproduction of any kind except where it pertains to short quotes in relation to advertising or promotion is strictly prohibited.

All Rights Reserved.

The characters and events portrayed in this book are fictitious. Any similarity to real persons, living or dead, is purely coincidental and not intended by the author.

ARE YOU SIGNED UP FOR DRAGONBLADE'S BLOG?

You'll get the latest news and information on exclusive giveaways, exclusive excerpts, coming releases, sales, free books, cover reveals and more.

Check out our complete list of authors, too!

No spam, no junk. That's a promise!

Sign Up Here

www.dragonbladepublishing.com

Dearest Reader;

Thank you for your support of a small press. At Dragonblade Publishing, we strive to bring you the highest quality Historical Romance from some of the best authors in the business. Without your support, there is no 'us', so we sincerely hope you adore these stories and find some new favorite authors along the way.

Happy Reading!

CEO, Dragonblade Publishing

Additional Dragonblade books by Author Mary Lancaster

Gentlemen of Pleasure
The Devil and the Viscount (Book 1)
Temptation and the Artist (Book 2)
Sin and the Soldier (Book 3)
Debauchery and the Earl (Book 4)

Pleasure Garden Series
Unmasking the Hero (Book 1)
Unmasking Deception (Book 2)
Unmasking Sin (Book 3)
Unmasking the Duke (Book 4)
Unmasking the Thief (Book 5)

Crime & Passion Series
Mysterious Lover
Letters to a Lover
Dangerous Lover

The Husband Dilemma Series
How to Fool a Duke

Season of Scandal Series
Pursued by the Rake
Abandoned to the Prodigal
Married to the Rogue
Unmasked by her Lover

Imperial Season Series
Vienna Waltz
Vienna Woods
Vienna Dawn

Blackhaven Brides Series
The Wicked Baron
The Wicked Lady
The Wicked Rebel
The Wicked Husband
The Wicked Marquis
The Wicked Governess
The Wicked Spy
The Wicked Gypsy
The Wicked Wife
Wicked Christmas (A Novella)
The Wicked Waif
The Wicked Heir
The Wicked Captain
The Wicked Sister

Unmarriageable Series
The Deserted Heart
The Sinister Heart
The Vulgar Heart
The Broken Heart
The Weary Heart
The Secret Heart
Christmas Heart

The Lyon's Den Connected World
Fed to the Lyon

De Wolfe Pack: The Series
The Wicked Wolfe
Vienna Wolfe

Also from Mary Lancaster
Madeleine

Chapter One

Rollo Darblay's life was unraveling.

He was very aware of that as he weaved his way to a comfortable-looking sofa in one of the Renwick Hotel's empty public rooms and set down the brandy bottle and glass on the table beside it. Having sloshed a decent measure into the glass, he folded himself onto the sofa to think.

This involved much focus on his brandy glass and a great deal of scowling. So, it was some time before he noticed the movement in the room and glanced up.

A golden lady shimmered in front of him and froze like a hunted deer before it bolts. As he blinked, the dazzling vision, probably caused by the array of candles behind her, resolved into a young lady wearing a charming evening gown of old gold silk. Her hair was not golden, but a dark blonde. He guessed her age to be just beyond twenty, and though her face lacked the kind of prettiness that usually attracted his roving attention, she was definitely pleasing to the eye. In a refined kind of way. She appeared to have been in the process of sneaking out of the room when he had looked up and caught her.

He grinned and rose to his feet with gratifying steadiness. "Don't leave on my account, ma'am. Utterly harmless, I assure you."

The lady unfroze into a much more regal posture, which for

some reason aroused his erratic chivalry.

"Have to tell you, though," he said severely, "you shouldn't be wandering around here alone."

Her eyebrows flew up. "My good sir, it is you who should not be here. This is the ladies' sitting room."

He blinked, then let out a crack of laughter. "Well, if that doesn't put the icing on my cake. I beg your pardon, ma'am, but you still shouldn't hang around here. There's a party of bosky fellows just across the hall."

A twinkle of amusement flashed in the lady's eyes. "Is there?" she marveled.

Which was when Rollo realized one could hear the clank of glasses and bursts of masculine laughter through the door he had left open. Nor was he blind to the irony of warning her against drunks, so he allowed an answering twinkle into his own eyes. "What the deuce is a ladies' sitting room anyway?"

"A place where ladies who might be traveling alone may sit and enjoy or ignore each other's company. There is usually a superior maid who sits by the door as chaperone, but I suppose it has grown late."

He frowned in fresh disapproval. "I hope *you* are not traveling alone."

"Indeed not. I am with a very respectable lady who retired early to bed—I think the journey has been too much for her—and I confess I was bored."

"Know the feeling," Rollo said sympathetically.

"You do not enjoy your own party?"

"Oh, I wasn't invited. I just joined them for a while, and they were amiable enough to welcome me. Didn't help, though."

"Didn't help what?" she asked.

Rollo sighed. "Devil of a day. I beg your pardon, deuce of a day. Join me?" He raised his glass.

"Ah, no, thank you. I don't believe that would be wise."

"True," Rollo allowed. "Well, at least sit down, then."

"I don't think that would be wise either."

Rollo considered. "Probably not. I'm not at all the thing, and I'm a trifle foxed besides. Still, if we're both bored, what harm is there in ten minutes' talk with the door open?"

"You make a persuasive case," the lady said gravely, although her eyes danced. Rather fine eyes that were neither green nor blue, but a brilliant combination of the two. Rollo began to like her. "Although since we have not been introduced…"

"Rollo Darblay," he said at once with a small bow, sincerely hoping she had never heard of him.

If she had, she was too polite to reveal her dismay. She gave the merest dip of a curtsey. "Gina Wallace."

"Gina is a pretty name."

"It's better than Virginia."

To his relief, she actually sat in the nearest chair—well, balanced somewhat nervously on the edge of it—and Rollo sank back onto the sofa with a sigh.

"What made your day so difficult?" she asked.

He scowled with fresh remembrance. "More than a day. Insoluble problems, Miss Wallace."

"Does brandy usually help them?"

His eyebrows flew up, and he was surprised into another breath of genuine laughter.

"I'm sorry," she said with what seemed to be genuine contrition. "I must sound like your mother."

"Lord, no, my mother would be the last to condemn me for drinking." He sighed, inclined to brood again. "Not a respectable family, sadly. Apart from Grace, which gives one hope."

"So, what brought you here to Renwick's Hotel?"

Nothing he said seemed to shock her, which was both endearing and challenging. So, he opted for the truth. "An assignation, but I might as well have stayed in town."

"Did she bore you?" Miss Wallace asked.

"Never got the chance to," Rollo admitted. "She never came. Sent a note she had decided to stay with some other fellow who's plumper in the pocket than your humble servant. Which is not difficult."

Her gaze swept over him. "You do not look like a poor man."

"No, well, that's part of the problem. Didn't know how deep the rot went until my father died."

"I'm sorry," she said quickly. "Did he die recently?"

"A month or so ago." He reached for his glass again and scowled at it. "And every day brings fresh revelations of doom. I came to escape, just for a day or two. Stupid, really, but there it is. What of you, Miss Wallace? Are you traveling to or from town?"

"To."

"To catch the rest of the Season?"

"Something like that." A rather sad little smile flickered across her lips and was gone. "Would it surprise you to know I am to be married?"

"Surprises me more you're not married already. Who's the lucky fellow?"

"I don't think I should tell you that until things are formalized."

Rollo fixed his eyes on her face. "Do you like him?"

"I barely know him. He is…older than I."

"Does that bother you?"

It was an odd question, so he wasn't surprised she looked startled. But she still answered. "Yes. It does. Wouldn't it bother you?"

Rollo gave a crooked smile. "Yes. It does. Why are you marrying him, then? Saving the family fortune?"

"On the contrary. My family aspires to the nobility."

"Not all it's cracked up to be," Rollo warned with a deprecating gesture to his person.

Her eyes widened again. "You are nobility?"

"Viscount. Stunning, is it not? Only recently inherited the title, of course. So, who are your people?"

She looked him in the eye. "Nouveau riche. My father owns cotton mills, with fingers in several other commercial pies."

Rollo's gaze fell to his glass, and at last, he knocked back half the contents. "My world looks down on those like you who aspire to nobility, but it doesn't stop us from seizing your wealth if we can get our greedy, superior mitts on it. I expect your world secretly looks down on us as over-proud wastrels, incapable of shifting for ourselves."

"Do you?" she asked.

"Do I what?" he asked, having lost his thread in contemplation of another idea.

"Look down on me?"

"Lord, no. Though I confess I'm not keen on the rich cits' daughters and widows paraded in front of me by my mother."

"Why not?"

"Well, one is a trifle long in the tooth, and the other some screeching schoolgirl. Don't misunderstand me—I'm no catch, and I'm sure they're estimable ladies, but the prospect of being married to either sent me straight to—" He broke off, remembering in the nick of time to whom he was speaking.

"To here," she finished for him, "and an assignation with someone more congenial."

He eyed her, a smile lingering on his lips for her understanding. "That was my plan. But like the others, it hasn't exactly worked out." His other idea popped back into his head. "Are you really bored, Miss Wallace?"

"Why?"

"Because straight from boredom to an unappealing marriage to please your family is no better for you than for me. And a short walk from the hotel is a pleasure garden." He glanced at the clock on the mantelpiece, since his watch had stopped working. "It is Saturday and not quite eleven, so we can even dance at the masked ball."

Miss Wallace, who had gradually relaxed into her chair as they talked, shot suddenly forward and glared at him. "Certainly not!"

THE YOUNG MAN had, so far, proved to be both unexpected and entertaining. He had sauntered into the room as if he owned it, totally ignoring her as he threw himself onto the sofa with an oddly boyish grace and proceeded to stare broodingly into his glass.

That was when he had taken her breath away, for there was nothing remotely boyish about his face, which was black-browed and dramatically handsome. In fact, he was the most beautiful male Gina had ever seen. Butterflies had soared in her stomach, both a pleasure and a warning. His dark, glittering eyes had told her he was not sober, and both his air and careless, expensive dress proclaimed him one of those entitled men of fashion she had been warned about.

So, although he had no right to be here, she had no intention of pointing it out. Instead, she had eased to her feet and crept toward the door. And when he had finally glanced up with confusion, she had been taken even further by surprise to glimpse a hint of sadness that amounted to despair.

That was what had frozen her to the spot. And been her undoing. Now he was inviting her to replace his absent mistress. But her outraged refusal did not quite have the effect she had imagined, even when she jumped angrily to her feet.

He only grinned and rose with her. "Don't get in a miff. I'm not offering to seduce you."

Heat flamed through her face. Seduced by *him*? Dear God, what would that entail? "Then what exactly *are* you offering?" she demanded.

"To escort you through a well-lit path in the gardens and dance," he said patiently. "If you don't care for the idea, don't come, but it would be more fun with you."

Back-footed again, she stared at him. No one had found her fun since childhood had vanished. "It would? Would you not rather dance with other females who might…" She broke off, blushing even more furiously. Heaven help her, what had she been about to say?

But the viscount's eyes merely danced with genuine amusement. "Other females who might be prepared to oblige me?" he suggested.

"Sir, you are a very improper person." Which, stupidly, intrigued rather than frightened her.

"I am," he allowed. "Going to the devil for years. Ask anyone. But you'll be quite safe with me. You remind me of my sisters."

For some reason, that didn't quite please her either.

"Besides," he added. "Notion's gone off me. Nothing like rejection to cool the ardor. Though I suppose I shouldn't be talking to you like that either."

"Nor to your sisters," she warned.

He appeared to think about that. "Don't think the topic's ever come up," he said at last. "Which is probably just as well because you're quite right."

"Are you a *rake*, sir?"

He shrugged. "Lord, I don't know. I'm told people usually call me a *rakehell*. I expect that's worse. Point is, never ruined anyone in my life, and not about to start."

"My lord, if I go anywhere alone with you, let alone to a pleasure garden ball, I will be ruined without your laying a finger on me."

"Not if you're not seen. And that's the beauty of the Maida balls. They're masked."

"Really?" She didn't mean to sound so intrigued, and it won her an encouraging grin from the reprobate opposite, who took a step closer.

"Really. The hotel will lend us domino cloaks and masks if we ask, and no one will be any the wiser."

A long-buried yearning for mischief, combined with a romantic notion of masquerade balls, threatened to overcome her natural wariness of a strange man who was a self-confessed rakehell. A rakehell who was already more than a trifle foxed.

And who hid, behind both concentrated scowls and the sparkle of youthful devilry, a profound sadness that spoke to her own. They were both desperate and under pressure to sacrifice themselves for family. Which was no reason to walk stupidly into the lion's den.

She refocused on his face to find him smiling ruefully down at her. He was intimidatingly tall, yet she had the feeling he didn't realize it. And in fact, she wasn't intimidated at all.

"Don't come if you'd rather not," he said gently. "I can finish my brandy with you instead or just leave you in peace in your ladies' sitting room."

And suddenly the thought of being left alone again with her silly novel and her dread of the future was intolerable.

"I'll come," she blurted, "but only for a little."

"We'll leave before the unmasking at midnight. Wait there."

Oddly, when he strode off, she didn't doubt her decision. In fact, as she paced the room, she was more uncertain about whether he would come back or be distracted again by the party he had just left. Although he was the most amiable drunk she had ever met, he was clearly not the steadiest of men.

I wonder if I would dare go alone to this masquerade? Just to see life, just to experience it before I am crushed by marriage and contempt...

"Here we are," the viscount said cheerfully, returning to the room with two domino cloaks over his arm and half-masks dangling from his long fingers. "I thought this yellow would suit your gown, though the mask is plain black." He dropped the yellow cloak over her shoulders and swung a plain black one over his own before handing her one of the masks.

With an odd, rising excitement, she placed the mask over her face and gazed through the eyeholes at her reflection in the wall mirror. She smiled in delight, swept back in time to simple childhood play, games of dressing up and pretending. For an hour, at least, she could be whoever she wanted to be, and she knew instinctively that the viscount would play along.

"Let me." He batted her fumbling fingers out of the way and tied the mask for her.

It was oddly disturbing to feel him so close behind her, his brisk fingers brushing against her hair. But there was nothing improper in his touch, and he stepped back immediately.

"Shall I return the favor?" she asked.

For an instant, she thought he hesitated, then he simply sank onto the nearest chair to make it easier for her to reach. His jet-black hair was unexpectedly soft to the touch. Soft and clean. Even with the faint whiff of alcohol on his breath, he smelled strangely pleasant.

He stood again as soon as she was finished. "Hood," he said significantly, and she hastily drew the hood of the cloak up over her head. Frowning, he adjusted it so that it covered her hair but did not fall over her entire face like a monk's cowl.

Then, with an exaggerated flourish that made her smile, he offered his arm. She laid her hand upon it, and they swept out of the sitting room and across the almost deserted front hall. The viscount's deserted friends still talked and laughed and clanked from a room on the far side. A dandy stood in the doorway, swaying gently. Lord Darblay didn't even look at him, merely thanked the liveried porter with the deft flip of a coin, and then they were in the fresh night air.

CHAPTER TWO

THERE WAS NOT much moonlight, although the weather was mild and dry. But the viscount had not misled her. Myriad lanterns lit the path from the hotel to the gardens.

"It can all be a bit improper by this time of the evening," the viscount said, "so if you're squeamish, keep your eyes on the path."

"Why?" she asked, inevitably intrigued, glancing into the gardens on either side. "What goes on there?"

A feminine squeal followed by a giggle and a masculine voice gave her a clue. She flushed, and the viscount said, "Told you. Don't worry, it's more civilized in the pavilion, though you might find it a little more…relaxed than you're used to."

"It's very pretty, though," she said, gazing further afield with some awe. The whole gardens were lit up with torches and lanterns that looked like fairy lights in the distance. Water from a fountain danced in the glow. Odd structures stood on shallow hills, a Grecian temple, an idealized castle. A waterfall cascaded from the highest of the hills. People in masks milled all over, flirting by the fountain, walking, dallying by the castle and the waterfall. All accompanied by distant waltz music.

It was like every fairytale, every imagining a child ever had. Gina was enchanted. They passed through the open doors into the pavilion.

"Later in the season, they dance outside," Lord Darblay said. "Every dance is a waltz, and strangers will ask you to stand up with them. It's considered impolite to refuse, so if you don't want to be bothered, stay close to me."

Gina was fascinated. She doubted there were many of the ton here, but clearly wealthy people rubbed shoulders, even danced with those of much poorer echelons of society. The prim and the vulgar danced together. Shopkeepers chatted up women in silk and jewels. And no one cared because they were all masked.

"What a wonderful idea," she breathed. "You could meet everyone here, find out about their lives and dreams."

"Maybe," he said, as she gazed about her. "But they'd probably make more sense if you came during the day."

"They have daytime dances, too?"

"An occasional tea dance, I think. But mostly, people just come to enjoy the gardens, a spot of rowing on the lake or playing with their children. You should have a look tomorrow before you go on to town."

"I will have to rise early. Mrs. Fitz is eager to get to town. If it wasn't for her headache, we would be there tonight. What are you…?"

Without warning, he had taken her hand and encircled her waist with his arm. He stepped closer, and she instinctively moved with him, only to be turned and swept to the left. They were on the dance floor, and they were waltzing.

"That was sudden," she said, covering her shock.

"Well, we came to dance."

And despite being not entirely sober, he danced divinely. All the natural grace she had seen even when he first threw himself onto the sofa of the ladies' sitting room was evident now in spades. He held her firmly, though no closer than was proper, and waltzed with a barely controlled exuberance that delighted her. He led with surprising deftness, especially considering his lack of sobriety, so he was easy to follow.

"There, I knew I'd like dancing with you," he remarked,

adding before she could even think of a reply. "Say when you want to sit down, for they barely pause between dances and it's not always clear where one starts and another begins."

"You have been here before."

"Often, especially when I was younger. I've been most places that society frowns on. Maida is pretty tame in the lists of dissipation but much more informal than ton parties, so it makes a pleasant change. Where did you say you came from?"

"Manchester. At least, I was born there, and that's where my father's business is largely located. We live in the country, now, a few miles outside the city."

"Don't you have pleasure gardens in Manchester?"

"Well, there is Tinker's," she said doubtfully, "but I have never been in the evening. I have walked there, occasionally, and listened to concerts, but I saw nothing like this. My father was very…protective."

"Then why don't you tell him you don't want to marry this man you barely know?"

"Because he protected me so that I *could* marry him. Or someone very like him. You won't understand, but someone like my father has no personal ambitions left except to have noble grandchildren."

"And you are to be sacrificed to those ambitions."

"You needn't say it like that. We all do our best for our families, do we not?"

"I suppose," he said grimly. "I never thought of my cits' daughters as sacrificing themselves. I want to marry them even less now."

"But then, you don't really want to marry at all, do you?" she asked shrewdly.

"No, I'm too interested in other things."

"Wine, women, and song?"

He looked surprised. "Lord, no, those are just moments, not interests. I have huge plans for the Darblay estates, which would make them profitable again, but I've got no money to implement such improvements. Instead, I'll have to sell some of the unentailed land just to pay off debts."

"Could you not mortgage some?"

"Mortgaged to the hilt already. I come from a long line of wastrels." He sounded so resigned that she gave him an encouraging smile.

"But you do dance excellently."

He grinned. "Do I? No one's ever told me that before. For what it's worth, so do you."

In perfect charity with each other, they danced on, sometimes in silence, sometimes talking of people glimpsed in the crowd or on the dance floor or little things totally unrelated to themselves or their surroundings. Since, despite his apparent reputation to the contrary, he was quite unthreatening company, she quickly relaxed and found him as entertaining as their initial encounter had promised.

And yet, behind her mask, she felt daring, mysterious, and sophisticated. The hour they had allowed passed in no time, without them sitting down once, and only when the music stopped and someone beneath the large clock at one end of the pavilion began to speak, did Gina realize it was a minute to midnight.

"Ladies and gentlemen," the master of ceremonies began.

"Quick, time to go," the viscount murmured, dropping his arm from her waist and spinning her toward the door. Hand-in-hand, they slipped through the crowd of excited revelers apparently thrilled with the anticipation of seeing their partners' faces.

Reaching a free passage to one of the doors, Lord Darblay began to run, and Gina ran with him, laughing with the uncomplicated joy of childhood. Once free of the pavilion, they slowed to a walk, listening to the distant shrieks and gasps from behind them.

"Close run thing," the viscount observed.

They walked through a sweetly scented garden, and Gina

sighed with contentment. "It's like another world here, where nothing else matters. I suppose that's the charm—to forget your troubles for a few hours. And perhaps get them in perspective."

"Have you?"

"There are people with worse problems."

She felt his gaze on her but didn't meet it. She realized he was still holding her hand loosely in his. For some reason, she liked it there, as though they were childhood friends going home after a day's play climbing trees and running wild around the woods. Somewhere, she was afraid that if she looked at him, the illusion would be destroyed. And yet, he was easy to look at. Even masked.

They reached the path to the hotel, and it was he who placed her hand on his arm in a more decorous position. "Keep the mask so no one sees you with me," he advised.

Reality intruded again, but at least she had a strange feeling that she no longer faced it alone.

In the entrance foyer, some of the party had spilled out of its bounds, but no one paid Darblay and Gina much attention. Someone did amble in front of them, but it was doubtful he even knew where he was going. The viscount gave him a gentle shove in the chest, and he landed on one of the comfortable sofas.

"Thanks, Rolls," came a faintly surprised voice from the cushions.

Gina's lips twitched, but she kept walking. "What about the masks and dominos?"

"Give me yours when we're private, and I'll take them back. Where are your rooms?"

"On the second floor." She was conscious of a desire to drag her feet, to keep company with him somewhere, somehow, for just a little longer. But that was foolish.

"These are our rooms," she murmured, pausing outside the middle door of the empty passage. She dropped his arm to seek the key in her reticule. Then she glanced up at him, which was a mistake.

He still wore his mask, which gave him something the look of a devil-may-care brigand, but his eyes were intent on her face, and for the first time, she sensed something other than easy friendship there. They were too warm, too…predatory. Suddenly, she felt hot all over, in the presence of the stranger she had once feared. She didn't feel frightened now. She didn't know what she felt, so hurried into speech.

"I'm sorry your lady friend let you down."

"I'm not. I've had a much pleasanter evening with you." He lifted his hands, unfastening her domino cloak, and suddenly she couldn't breathe. His knuckles brushed softly against the bare skin of her throat. He drew off the cloak, then reached around her head to tug the strings of her mask. How did he smell so good? Warm, clean male, spice and cut grass…

Determinedly, she thrust out her hand. *Don't you dare invite me to your rooms. Oh, God, please do…*

He took her hand. "If I can ever help, I will. Good luck, my enchantress." To her amazement, he raised her hand and brushed his lips across her knuckles.

And then he was striding away along the passage to the staircase, leaving her to stumble inside alone.

ROLLO BREATHED A sigh of relief as he fell onto his own bed. He had come close, but somehow, he had retained enough sense—or at least honor—not to seduce her. But, God, he wanted her. She was so sweet and had felt so delightful in his arms. A beautiful woman who neither feared him nor expected anything of him. A girl who laughed with him and shared his appreciation of the ridiculous.

On the walk home, he had been aware of a reluctance to part with her, a desire to know more and more about her, what made her happy, what her life was like, what she wished it to be, everything. Which had been odd in itself, for normally, he didn't much care for chattering girls. But Gina Wallace didn't chatter to fill a silence, to build up to demands or complaints. She just said what was in her heart, and he found that truly endearing. And toward her, he had felt the same sort of protectiveness he felt toward his sisters. Like wanting to scare off the unknown nobleman who'd been "bought" by her rich family.

Only the realization that they stood outside her bedchamber had made him aware of the stirrings of his body. And she wasn't immune. He had flustered her. He was sure she, too, had felt the tug of attraction and desire. And this would definitely be the only opportunity.

Rollo liked women. And since they tended to like him, he had gone through life happily taking what he chose from what was offered. But they were all women who understood the game—ladybirds or married women of the ton who took a shine to him. Debutantes and young unmarried females were generally too well warned against him to be anything but either awed or frightened, and most of them were a dead bore in any case. Unmarried girls of respectable families had never tempted him before.

He sat up, frowning, and reached for the pitcher of water beside the bed. While he drank it down without bothering about the glass beside it, he made another discovery. His disturbing urge to take Gina Wallace to bed had not just been about his own desires. He had wanted to give her something to make her happy. A little pleasure before she faced the dull sacrifice of a duty marriage to an old man. She was not the sort of woman to break her marriage vows. This would have been her one chance to choose, and he would have done everything in his not quite sober power to bring her a little joy.

But even that would have been unkind.

He rose, tore off his clothes, and washed in cold water. Another means of cooling the ardor. Then he threw himself back into bed and stared up at the ceiling, seeing her laughing eyes and her dazzling smile. And tortured himself by remembering the feel of her in his arms, the subtle scent of her hair, her skin, by imagining how she would look naked and undone in his arms, flushed with passion... And drifted, eventually, into dreams he could not control.

UNFORTUNATELY, HE WOKE to reality. Which, for Rollo, was a slightly sore head and the prospect of proposing to either Miss Gush or Mrs. Take-me-as-I-am. Like Gina Wallace, he would just have to bite the bullet and do his duty. His father's debts would be paid, along with his own. The estates would be saved, the land improved, and all the people who depended on him, from his mother to the lowliest farm tenant and servant, would be not only saved from penury, but their positions improved. His sister Hope would have a dowry.

Surely, marriage was a small price to pay for such universal contentment? Certainly, it would be a huge weight off his mind and heart. And no sane person would expect him to be a good husband and never stray.

Irritably, he rang for the hotel servant and ordered a large pot of coffee. While he waited, he finished the pitcher of water and rose from his bed. Naked, he paced to the window and scowled out onto the front drive of the hotel. A traveling coach was being loaded up with baggage by a small army of servants. He wondered if it was Miss Wallace and her chaperone. Well, it wasn't as if he could wave to her right now, so he backed off and stuck his head in the washing bowl instead.

While drinking several cups of coffee, he dressed in decent buff pantaloons, a perfectly fitting blue coat, and a snowy white cravat, casually tied and fixed with a plain gold pin. All his other jewels had been sold or pawned, apart from one opal ring that was next in line.

He dragged the comb through his hair, poured the remains of

his coffee into the cup, and stared broodingly out of the window.

Time to grow up, Rolls. Do the right thing and make the most of it.

But first, a brisk walk to blow away the last of the cobwebs.

He set down the empty cup and made his way downstairs. He thought of inquiring of the staff if Miss Wallace had left, but he had no reason to ask such a thing, and it didn't really matter. So, he strode out of the building, ignoring a crowd of young men with sorer heads than his, and set off not to the pleasure garden but to the open country beyond the hotel.

It might be fun, he thought, just to keep walking, become someone else and see where he ended up. Let others sort out the viscountcy. Cousin Thomas could surely do a better job than his poor old father.

But not better than you, Rolls. You know how to make it work. All you need is the money to start.

With fresh determination, he spun on his heels and began to stride back the way he had come. His newly polished boots were splashed with mud, but such sartorial misdemeanors had never bothered him. It was time to deal with reality.

Except, when he strode up to the front door, an elegant lady in a blue walking dress and matching spencer walked out of it. She wore a rather fetching cream bonnet trimmed with blue ribbons. And beneath the brim was a face that stopped his heart.

She saw him at the same moment, and a surprised smile lit up her face, turning it from merely pleasing to dazzlingly beautiful. "My lord!"

"Miss Wallace." He bowed, trying to gather his wits while he glanced around for the chaperone. "I thought I had missed you. Are you about to set off?"

She wrinkled her nose. "No, just for a walk. Mrs. Fitzwilliam is still under the weather and remains in bed. She may rally by the afternoon, but she is already talking about staying for another night." She glanced around her as though to be sure of privacy on the empty terrace. "I saw your friends depart. In quite a sorry state."

Rollo grinned. "Rank amateurs in the art of dissipation."

"Then you are not suffering?"

"Devil a bit. Which is why, if you summon your maid, I can offer to escort you on a walk in the pleasure garden." So much for going home and doing his duty. Well, what difference did a few hours make?

She hesitated, a hundred expressions chasing across her face so quickly that he couldn't read them. "There is no need, sir."

"No, but if you want the company, I am happily at your disposal. I can, equally, keep out of your way if you prefer solitude." He smiled to show he wasn't remotely hurt by her lack of enthusiasm.

To his surprise, her eyes lightened at once and she smiled again. "Actually, I would be glad of the company. And since Mrs. Fitz requires two maids to wait on her, mine is fully occupied."

CHAPTER THREE

GINA WAS UNPREPARED for the rush of happiness that struck her as soon as she saw him. And then a thousand tiny fears flitted through her mind, the chief of which was that he would not recognize her, that he would be embarrassed to meet her, or that he would simply give her the cut direct. Last night he had been drunk and amiable. This morning, in the sober light of day, she had no idea what she would face.

Astonishment. An austere offer to escort her—with her maid—to walk in the gardens. And then, at her hesitation, a suddenly vulnerable boy, unexpectedly easy to hurt. Which meant his offer had been genuine, and her euphoria rushed back.

She took his proffered arm. "Mrs. Fitzwilliam informed me I would meet no one who matters in the gardens at this time of the morning."

"She's probably right. Never been before midday myself. Have you breakfasted?"

"Yes, we had it sent to our rooms. So how do you avoid the sorry mornings after? My brother, who is only eighteen but should know better, sits with a damp cloth around his head until luncheon, will eat nothing, and growls all day like a bear with a sore tooth."

"So would I with a damp cloth around my head for hours. Surprised he doesn't catch a lung fever."

"So, what would you recommend?"

He glanced at her with a smile playing around his sensual lips. She had lain awake last night, wondering how those lips would feel on hers. She still wondered, and so did the butterflies dancing in her stomach.

"Copious amounts of clean water before bed," he said, "and lots of coffee in the morning, followed by fresh air and a decent breakfast."

"You sound very certain."

"I've had a lot of practice. But then, a friend of mine swears by tea and a huge breakfast before leaving his chamber. Each to their own. Why are we discussing something so improper for young ladies?"

They wandered into the pleasure gardens. The sun winked out from behind a cloud, bringing a welcome warmth.

"Curiosity is my besetting sin," Gina confessed.

"You mean you never stole into your father's study as a child to try his brandy?"

"We never had it in the house until my brother went up to university. Why, is that what you did?"

"I've a vague recollection of Grace and me doing it on a couple of occasions. It didn't take much to make her giggle, and I had to smuggle her out before we got caught. It was easier at school."

"School!"

He grinned. "I was a bad boy, always being sent home for some misdemeanor or other."

"Did your parents look at you as though you were a sad disappointment to them?"

He considered. "No. Not sure my mother actually noticed, beyond being pleased to see me, and my father seemed to regard it as a source of pride and amusement in equal measure."

The smile in his eyes died slowly.

"Do you miss him badly?" she asked.

"Oddly, I do. Apart from our mighty disagreements, we had little enough to do with each other, and he wasn't much of a guiding light. But we did laugh sometimes. And he was *there*."

Gina nodded. "My mother was a bit of a Puritan, and we always rubbed each other up the wrong way, but she was always there, too."

He nodded as though he understood. "But more of the guiding light, I imagine."

"Not as much as she should have been," Gina said ruefully. "I was a wayward child."

"When did she die?"

"Oh, years ago. I was fourteen, Jason was ten, and the girls eight. I am used to running a household, which is one reason Lord…" She broke off, realizing what she had almost said. "Oh, look, this is pretty!"

They had come upon a quiet grove with a swing on its edge. She sat in it, more to distract him, for she thought he would gallantly push it for her. He didn't. He sat in it beside her and casually swung his legs to make it move.

"Your promised husband?" he said. "You might as well tell me about him."

In fact, she could see no reason not to. They seemed to have fallen back very quickly into the manner of friends. "He is a…mature gentleman. His manners are perfect."

"Lord…?" he prompted.

"Longton," she said, giving up.

His breath hissed. "Longton?"

"You know him?" she asked uneasily.

"He was a friend of my father's."

Somehow, she didn't like the suddenly grim look in his eye. "Is he not as amiable as he appeared when he visited us?"

"Oh, he's amiable enough. And old enough not to go picking up brides younger than his daughters."

"I am two-and-twenty," she said with dignity. "And, therefore, past my first flush of youth."

"We can share walking sticks in another year or two."

"You don't like Lord Longton," she observed.

Darblay shrugged impatiently. "I don't dislike him."

"Then what?"

His smile was crooked. "If he was younger, we might move in the same circles. But then, I believe he has calmed down recently. He may well make you a decent husband."

It was all she had hoped for when she had left home. But now, something she didn't want to think about was churning inside her, and she had to squash it ruthlessly. "What about your prospective brides? Who are they?"

"Miss Gush and Mrs. Take-me-as-you-find me," he said absently.

She smiled. "Their real names!"

His black brows lifted. "Actually, I don't remember."

A choke of shocked laughter escaped her. "And you're planning to marry one of them?"

He sighed. "Yes."

"Then which holds your grudging favor?"

"I haven't decided, yet."

"Well, when you do, I advise you to learn her name before you make your offer. And don't let the nickname slip out by mistake."

He grinned. "I am quite out of line, I know. Between ourselves, they're not the type of women I usually admire."

"Well, you can't marry your ladybird," she said reasonably, and this time it was his shout of laughter that disturbed the peace.

"You can't go around saying things like that," he warned. "It will put old Longton into a huff."

"I must not notice his ladybirds." She meant it to be light, but it came out rather desolately instead.

Darblay took her hand in a comforting squeeze, and she realized suddenly that the gentle movement of the swing had brought them closer together. His thigh actually rested against hers, warm and muscular. A pulse leapt in her throat.

"*Could* you like him?" Darblay asked.

No one had actually asked her that before. "He is an interesting dinner companion." Her breath caught, and she jumped to her feet. "Shall we walk on?"

She didn't want to think about Lord Longton, let alone talk about him, in this bonus few hours of freedom she had been granted. Fortunately, the viscount seemed to sense that and changed the subject by imitating various bird songs about them. He possessed a rather fine baritone voice, so the lowering of the bird's cheeps made her laugh. Eventually, she joined in, making up words for the songs, which made him laugh. And when they got into a shouting match with the crows, they both laughed, along with a growing array of small children who had appeared from nowhere.

Eventually, they left the children making up their own bird songs and found themselves by some tables and chairs where a few people were drinking tea or eating sandwiches under a canopy.

"Breakfast," the viscount said with relish and invited her to precede him. A young woman in a cap and apron smiled hugely and showed them to a table.

"What would you like?" he asked Gina.

"Perhaps just a cup of tea. It's not long since I ate."

"We have freshly baked scones, ma'am," the waitress told her proudly. "Still warm from the oven."

"We'll have some of those," Lord Darblay said, "Along with tea and a plate of ham and eggs and toast."

It seemed delightfully strange and daring to be eating alone in public with a man. A very attractive man. Gina was not blind to the admiring glances and surreptitious stares of the waitress, female patrons at other tables, and even passersby. Lord Darblay himself, however, seemed quite oblivious. He smiled at the waitress who brought their food, almost causing the poor girl to swoon, but otherwise paid attention only to Gina.

And to his food, of course, which he ate with enthusiasm but perfect manners, before sitting back in satisfaction and reaching for his tea.

"Better?" Gina asked humorously.

"Quite set up. I need to walk it off now. Do you want to wander a bit more? The gardens are filling up, and there will probably be jugglers and stilt-men and so on."

"And music?"

"In the afternoon, certainly. If the rain stays off, they hold concerts in the rose garden at midday. Are you musical?"

"I enjoy music. Don't you?"

"I can appreciate it. Except for opera. Sopranos hurt my ears with their caterwauling, especially the ones who can't stay on the dashed note. They have a particularly fine harpist here."

They spent another enjoyable hour wandering the gardens, watching jugglers, who were a great draw to the children, as were the men and women on stilts who joked and clowned around from their massive height.

At last, Gina said reluctantly. "I should go back and see how Mrs. Fitzwilliam goes on. And I suppose you will want to get back to town."

"I should," he admitted. "I'll walk back with you and throw my things in a bag."

"How did you come out here?"

"Hackney."

"Perhaps you could come with us in the carriage."

He cast her a sardonic glance. "I wouldn't suggest that to your Mrs. Fitzwilliam."

"I suppose not," she agreed. "Too many awkward questions."

They walked on toward the hotel in companionable if slightly sad silence. She liked the way he moved beside her, all restless, somehow reckless elegance. She felt curiously protected by his large form, his friendship.

And yet they could not really be friends. Circumstances had thrown them together, but they barely knew each other. That fact did not slow her growing physical awareness of him. Last night, foxed, he had been charming and just a little dangerous. Enough to appeal to her own dormant recklessness. Sober, and in the sunshine, he presented a much more subtle yet intense danger. His carelessly wicked smile disturbed her, his lightest, casual touch excited her in ways she couldn't grasp, ways that felt nothing like friendship.

But whatever these confused feelings were, they would be gone in moments, along with him...

"Let me know if you're staying for the rest of the day," he said abruptly. "We can go and hear the music if you like."

Her heart lightened as though someone had thrown a lever. "How will I find you?"

"I'll be in the rose garden."

She nodded, and since there were people alighting from a carriage outside the hotel, she merely curtseyed in return to his bow and hurried inside.

What if I never see him again? What if that is the last thing he remembers of me? Or I him? A civil bow. An indifferent curtsey... It didn't matter, of course. She would always have the fun of last night's dancing and this morning in the garden.

She found Mrs. Fitzwilliam propped up in bed by a mass of pillows, drinking some cordial prepared for her by her devoted maid. Little, Gina's maid, was reading to her.

"Oh, there you are, Gina," Mrs. Fitzwilliam said weakly. "I am so sorry. This must be so dull for you, to be stuck so close to town but not yet there and with no company."

"The gardens are very pleasant, ma'am. I have enjoyed walking after so many days trapped in the coach. How are you feeling?"

"As weak as a kitten, my dear. I swear I have absolutely no energy, though my headache is a little better."

"Well, that is something. I suppose the rattling of the coach must be responsible for your poor head."

"It is true I am always laid low by a journey," Mrs. Fitzwilliam mourned.

"Perhaps," Gina suggested, "we should stay another night until you are feeling more the thing. Then the short journey tomorrow should not trouble you."

Feeling rather guilty about her attempted manipulation, Gina awaited the older woman's decision with bated breath.

"No," Mrs. Fitzwilliam decided. "I could not keep you from town another day. Your family has entrusted you to me for the purpose—"

"Certainly not for the purpose of making you ill, ma'am! My father would be appalled to think you had made yourself more ill for such a paltry reason. For his sake as well as mine, you should not travel any further until you are quite recovered."

"Oh. Do you think so, my dear?" Mrs. Fitzwilliam asked hopefully.

"Miss Gina is quite right," declared Colton, Mrs. Fitzwilliam's maid, bustling into the room. "Have you drunk up all that cordial?"

Shortly after, Mrs. Fitzwilliam was settled down for a nap, and Gina slipped away to her own chamber to repair her hairpins and splash a little water on her face and hands.

"Do you not want a nap, miss?" Little said, replacing the loosened pins. "Especially since you were so late to bed."

"No," Gina said uncompromisingly. "I have too much energy to sit still. I am going to go out again and listen to the music in the garden."

"I should come with you," Little said morosely. She was not much interested in the outdoors, except in so far as it affected her mistress's clothing.

"We're not in town, yet, Little," Gina assured her. "I shall be quite safe in the garden for an hour or so." With that, she stood, redonned her hat and spencer, and sallied forth to the rose garden with unholy glee.

Lord Darblay was exactly where he had said he would be, leaning against a hedge just inside the rose garden, moodily picking the petals off a fallen rosebud. Her heart thudded. When he saw her, a slow smile curved his lips, and as he straightened and walked toward her, she realized with awe that he really was pleased to see her. He wasn't just being kind.

For a little, they stood together, listening, while Gina gazed around the garden.

Several rows of chairs had been laid out in front of the makeshift platform where the musicians played. Though the concert had begun with rather dignified chamber music, the audience appeared to be quite fluid, with only a few people maintaining their seats. Others came, sat, and went again, to be replaced by others wandering past. Everyone seemed to be dressed in their Sunday best, mostly middling sort of folk with a scattering of the obviously poorer among them.

One man entering the garden caught her attention by his straight, military bearing, although he wore the civilian dress of a gentleman. He also had one empty coat sleeve pinned to his shoulder. Without looking to right or left, he sat on the end of a row, just as the music came to an end and the orchestra took a bow.

Lord Darblay seized her arm and urged her along the hedge toward the back of the seats.

"Do you know that man?" Gina whispered.

"Lord Richard Gorse. Old army officer, lost his arm at Waterloo. His brother's a friend of mine, so I don't want him seeing me with you. Not that he goes out much, and he's hardly a gossip by nature. Wonder what he's doing here?"

"Perhaps he likes music."

The viscount ushered her to a seat in the back row and lounged beside her. How could a man look so disreputably careless, and yet so elegant at the same time? He took her breath away.

The orchestra was welcoming a demurely dressed young woman to the stage. She walked on quietly and sat behind a harp. With her first note, the audience quieted, and Gina had the immediate impression that here was something special.

The music was almost heavenly. Gina listened in awe, aware of nothing else, except, as a subtly thrilling background that merged with the music, the firm warmth of Lord Darblay's arm against hers. Only when the music came to a soft, tragic end, did she draw in a deep breath and surreptitiously wipe her gloved finger across the corner of her eye.

Darblay was not watching the stage. He was watching her. And the expression in his eyes, though she didn't understand it, caused those butterflies in her stomach to dive sharply, depriving her of air all over again.

Time seemed to stop. Then his fingers closed around hers and her heart thudded. *What in the world is…?*

A soprano's voice rang out over the renewed harping, and Darblay sprang up from his seat, dragging Gina with him. Charging past the plump couple on the end of their row, he muttered an apology and bolted for the gate.

Brimming with uncontrollable laughter, she ran with him, out of the gate and along the path.

"Told you," Darblay said, pausing with a grin at last. "Can't stand the screeching. Hope you weren't enjoying it too much."

"I enjoyed the harpist. She's *very* good."

"Do you want to go back? I can stick some grass in my ears."

Gina laughed again. "You would, too, wouldn't you? No, let's do something else."

"The pond is this way. We could take out a boat if you like."

They did. Darblay handed over a penny for the privilege and climbed into a small rowing boat before handing her in. She sat on the wooden bench while Darblay took off his coat and rowed them around the artificial pond, carefully avoiding the other two boats out at the same time.

Watching his easy strength stirred something within her. When his shirt plastered itself to his skin and she could see the play of his muscles, the feeling sharpened. *I like him. But this is more. This is…desire. Unladylike, physical desire. What is wrong with me?*

Shocked by the insight, she looked away, at anything other than him. *He is my friend. He is the kind of man—*

Not the *kind* of man. *The* man she might have wanted to court her, to marry her. She had never felt such physical tumult before, and now she would never know its outcome. There would only be Lord Longton, more than twice her age, stout and sagging with over-indulgence. She had thought she could bear it, endure it…

"Gina?" Lord Darblay had stopped rowing, frowning at her in concern. "What is it?"

"I… Is there no way out for you, other than to marry an heiress you do not like?"

His hands fell away from the oars. "I haven't met one I do like who'd be prepared to marry me. Everyone knows my family's circumstances. It's never been a secret. No wellborn girl would be allowed to marry me. The only people who would benefit from an alliance with me are the nouveau riches who are prepared to buy their way into nobility."

"Like me," she said bleakly.

He locked the oars and moved to sit on the bench beside her. There was scarcely room, and the boat tipped alarmingly, but he didn't seem to notice. "Not like you," he said firmly. "Like your family maybe. I suppose we are both being sold, but at least I have nominal control over whom I sell myself to."

"Will you bear it?"

"I'll have to. Will you?"

She gave him an unhappy smile. "I'll have to. It's different for men, though, isn't it? Will you still have your ladybirds?"

He didn't even laugh this time. "In all honesty, I probably will. Light relief. The best I could be, once I have an heir or two, is a complaisant, straying husband. My best hope is for a tolerable, cordial marriage."

"But that isn't what you always wanted, is it?"

"Never thought of it," he said ruefully. "I lived in the present, mostly. When I went to Oxford, I was desperate for a pair of colors, to fight under Wellington. My father wouldn't hear of it, so I sulked and went to the devil. Then I developed an interest in the science of agriculture and realized how we could save the estates, but my father wouldn't hear of it from a brainless wastrel like me, even when my brother-in-law and his stewards vouched for me. So, I carried on to the devil. I knew, in theory, I would have to marry one day, but until the old man curled up his toes... I'll be a terrible husband. I shouldn't complain about a less than perfect wife."

He was silent, gazing down at her until she looked up. "Who did *you* want to marry? Is there someone Longton is taking you from?"

"No." Her breath caught. "Yes. But I don't think I could marry someone and stray."

He raised one hand, touching her cheek with the backs of his fingers. "No, you wouldn't. You could elope."

"And shame myself and my family? Ruin the chances of my sisters who are depending on me. And Lord Longton."

He leaned into her. "It's a muddle. We can still be friends. If you like."

Her heart warmed and she smiled. "I do like." His face was so close to hers, that she could kiss him. What would his lips feel like on hers? How did he kiss? With more grace, she knew instinctively, than the fumbling slobbers she had occasionally been treated to in her youth.

He bent nearer, and for a wondrous, terrible moment, she thought he *would* kiss her. Her heart seemed to dive with all those butterflies.

"Damn, I'm going to sink us," he said and heaved himself back to the rowing bench. But he wasn't embarrassed. As he took up the oars again, he smiled at her, and she smiled back, as a daring, shocking, wonderful idea began to form in her mind.

Chapter Four

"Is THERE NO way out for you, other than to marry an heiress you do not like?"

"I haven't met one I do like."

Except he had. Gina's question had forced him to acknowledge the truth—that he would easily have chosen her over all of them. Over anyone. *Her* money would save the estates. *He* was nobleman enough to keep her family happy, even if he wasn't an earl. And he would be content, happy. He wouldn't even stray. Probably. And he would do his best to make *her* happy, with far more chance than old Longton.

But even if it wasn't official, her family had made the bargain with Longton and would stick to it. Her family probably could not afford the scandal of jilting one's betrothed, not like a lady of his own class. Except the betrothal was not yet public. If Longton had been shouting about it, more fool him. Let him find another heiress.

In the grip of more hope than he could remember since his brother-in-law had let him "apprentice" himself to his steward, Rollo pulled on the oars, speeding them around the lake, until he noticed what he was doing and slowed.

Could he convince her? What would she say if he asked her to marry him instead of Longton? Would it ruin their friendship? Would she be so offended that she'd storm off? He couldn't imagine the latter, but one never knew with women, and although Gina Wallace was different from any other woman he'd met, he had not known her a full day.

Do I really want to do this?

God, yes.

He wanted her very badly. And for more, much more than an afternoon of sweet diversion.

He opened his mouth to speak her name.

"My lord," she said decisively.

"Rollo," he corrected. "I think we're familiar enough for that."

A funny little smile flickered across her face and vanished. "Rollo. Would you mind if I asked you a rather personal and quite improper question?"

"Have at me," he invited, intrigued.

Color deepened along her delicate cheekbones. Her fingers pleated nervously at her gown. "I think you are a man who has a good deal of experience with women," she said in a rush.

"I'm flattered you might think so," he said, startled, "but—"

"You have at least one ladybird—"

"Had," he interrupted.

"...And I doubt she was the first or the only. I am not judging you," she added hurriedly, "it just seems to make you the right person to ask."

Rollo stopped rowing again. "About what?"

"Intimacy," she said, blushing fierily from her forehead to where the base of her throat vanished inside her spencer. "Between a man and a woman. I suppose it must be enjoyable, else you would not do so much of it?"

Rollo, torn between laughter and acute discomfort, managed to say breathlessly, "Yes, but you shouldn't be talking to me about these things."

"Yes, for *men*," she pursued. "But... Can women enjoy it, too?"

She was scared. Scared of marriage, especially with such a

specimen as Longton, and she had no mother, no married sisters to confide in.

"Most definitely." But would she enjoy physical intimacy with Longton? No one could say the man had no experience, but he was hardly love's young dream. The whole idea made Rollo feel ill, so God knew what it was doing to her. "Gina—"

"Then I have a favor to ask you," she blurted. "Would you show me?"

He stared at her. In fact, he was very afraid he goggled, which can't have done much for his attraction either. He swallowed. "You want me to make love to you?"

"If you wouldn't mind." She was gazing down at the demented pleating of her gown. "I have been led to believe that men are less *picky* than women, but—"

"Jesus Christ, Gina!"

She closed her eyes, so clearly covered in shame for what she had asked and what she probably saw as his rejection. He locked the oars in place, abandoned them once again, and risked capsizing by joining her on the bench. This time, lest there be any doubt, he flung his arm around her shoulders and hugged her to his side.

"Gina, any man would be honored, delighted beyond words to be welcomed into your bed. But think what you are offering." And to whom. Longton might be older and fatter, but Rollo was hardly a catch either. Gina deserved better than either of them.

"I will do it," she said in a small, hard voice. "I will marry Longton, and I will be a good and faithful wife to him. But I am not a stone, Rollo. If I make all the sacrifices, should I not know a little happiness first? Before I am tied for life to another man? If I am worth that, then I would like it to be with you. If you don't dislike the idea."

Rollo's anatomy approved the idea enthusiastically. His mind was speechless.

"Would he know?" she asked.

Rollo scowled. "Not from me! For God's sake, Gina—"

"No, I mean…on our wedding night. Would he be able to tell that I was not…"

"A virgin?" Rollo said bluntly. "Not necessarily. There are many reasons a hymen may not remain intact." And he doubted Longton would care. Since she was still reluctant to look at him, he pushed up her chin so that he could see her face. "You are very trusting," he said helplessly. "No one has ever trusted me before."

"Why not?"

He shrugged. "Because I am not a good man. I'm going to the devil and everyone knows it." Making love to Gina would send him even farther along that path, cross yet another line, for he had never yet deflowered a virgin. The really bizarre part was, as he gazed into her eyes, it felt more like redemption.

"You *are* a good man," she said stoutly. "You, too, are making a sacrifice. And maybe you can find a little happiness with me first."

"Oh Gina," he groaned. "Where do you get these strange ideas? I should row you straight back and return you to your Mrs. Fitz before I do something we'll both regret."

"Is it against your honor?" she asked anxiously.

"No." He dropped his forehead against hers. "It's against yours."

With the softness of a butterfly's wing, her fingertips touched his cheek, his lips, and he couldn't breathe. "No," she whispered. "It will give me courage I didn't know I needed."

This time it was Rollo who closed his eyes, fighting his desire not only for her body but to please her, to make things easier for her. Had he not already offered to help her if he could?

"Would it really help?"

She nodded, her forehead sliding against his.

Rollo sent up a prayer, his first for many a year and entirely wordless. He touched his lips to hers. Silk and fire, sweetness and astonishment. He couldn't allow himself to linger or he would devour her. "Then how do we manage this?"

She swallowed and drew back. "I can come to your rooms

when everyone is asleep. They retire early."

He heaved himself back to the oars. "You can still change your mind. I will understand."

"So can you," she said generously, then with a quick, half-frightened glance. "Do you think you will?"

He could lie and be free of this temptation, go and get drunk with his friends in town. Or he could be as honest as she. "No. I won't."

>>><<<

HE DIDN'T TREAT her differently after her shocking proposal. There was no lack of respect as he handed her out of the boat, no disgust when he offered his arm to walk on through the gardens. In fact, she thought he was deliberately amusing her until she recovered something of her old comfort in his presence.

But she could hardly forget what she had asked of him. And his big, elegant person strolling along beside her only filled her veins with anticipation and excitement.

She was going to be wicked for the first time in her life. She was going to enjoy every last moment of it.

And then, she would be good for the rest of her life, with the memory of Rollo Darblay buried in her heart.

"It is almost teatime," she said. "I should go back to Mrs. Fitzwilliam and take my turn reading to her, at least. I... I have not appalled you, have I?"

They were on one of the higher paths among the trees, deserted at this time. Even so, Rollo glanced up and down before drawing her behind a tree.

"Never think it," he said, almost harshly, dragging her hand to his heart. "You make my heart sing. And when we meet again...I will not be a *polite* lover. But I will make your whole being dance with pleasure—or die trying."

Before she could respond, she was crushed in his arms, and

his mouth came down on hers.

Nothing had prepared her for such a kiss, not even the sensual, butterfly brush of his lips in the boat. Nor was there anything remotely fumbling or slobbery about it. Instead, his mouth was firm, warm, and urgent—and curiously elegant, like Darblay himself. The kiss blended with his embrace, his body pressed to hers, giving her a taste of his muscular strength, the hard ridge of his arousal, his passion. And hers, for everything in her leapt in helpless response. *"I will make your whole being dance with pleasure..."* Dear God, what had she taken on?

Her body had no such fears. It was pushing back against him with delight, and her arms were around his neck, her hands caressing his nape, fisting in his hair.

And then it was over. His mouth and his arms loosened. While she gazed up at him in bemusement, he straightened her bonnet and tucked an escaped lock of hair beneath it.

"Until tonight," he murmured in her ear, and then he was gone.

For several seconds, she stared stupidly after him as he sauntered back down the path. She touched her lips in awe, and they smiled beneath her fingers. *Oh, my. Oh, my goodness...*

Giving herself a brisk little shake, she stepped around the tree, back onto the path, and walked in the opposite direction to Rollo, toward the hotel gate. Her whole being was already singing.

GINA PASSED THE rest of the day in an unprecedented state of excitement, nerves, and anticipation. While she drank tea with Mrs. Fitzwilliam, read to her, and dined quietly in their private sitting room, Lord Darblay was never far from her thoughts.

She decided halfway through the rather tasty fish course that she must always have been rather wicked. Because she had made an assignation with a man, just like Rollo's ladybird, only Gina had every intention of keeping hers. She was not even ashamed. This was a mere treat she was allowing herself before the rest of her life, a marriage she did not care to think about but which she would make the best she could.

And her treat harmed no one. She felt no sense of betrayal toward Lord Longton, who wanted only her money and her body to provide an heir. He had not even proposed to her personally, merely come to her father's home to look her over like a horse. His manners had been genial, respectful enough, but she had felt almost superfluous to requirements. Marriage had been discussed between Longton and her father and an agreement was made. She would travel to London where the betrothal was to be made formal. She would be introduced to society, and her father would join them for the wedding ceremony.

Gina was bound by her father's agreement, but she herself had accepted nothing, promised nothing. She would, of course, because anything else was unthinkable, but for this day, a small, rebellious part of her that had always found the arrangement of her life infamous seemed to have risen up with relish and taken over.

She was grateful to Rollo Darblay. Without him, she would never have thought of this treat… At least, she hoped it would be a treat. Anticipation and nerves made it hard to concentrate on either dinner conversation or the game of cards that followed. Fortunately, Mrs. Fitzwilliam was much recovered and chattered for both of them. She was looking forward to a leisurely drive into town tomorrow, in time, perhaps to pay a few calls and join the throngs in Hyde Park where, apparently, one had to be seen at five of the clock.

Gina agreed to everything with an amiable smile. She would be a different person by then. She would have a secret she would never tell, a precious, few moments with a man who brought her fun and laughter, who made her heart flutter and her knees weak with his kiss. And she would not, could not, think beyond that.

Before retiring, Mrs. Fitzwilliam decided on a gentle walk

around the hotel grounds. Gina, donning her hat and a warm cloak to accompany her, both hoped and feared to glimpse Lord Darblay prowling nearby.

"The grounds are pretty." Mrs. Fitzwilliam sounded surprised. "Is this where you walked all day?"

"No, mostly in the pleasure garden, which is just over there. The gardens are lovely, and there was music to listen to, jugglers to watch."

Mrs. Fitzwilliam sniffed. "I always heard Maida was even more vulgar than Vauxhall or Ranelagh. But the hotel is very comfortable, don't you think?"

It was also, fortunately, quiet, since few travelers had arrived on a Sunday. There were no raucous parties spilling into the foyer, and the ladies' sitting room contained only two spinster ladies drinking tea. After a civil conversation, the spinsters began to put away their needlework, and Mrs. Fitzwilliam pronounced herself ready for bed.

Gina dutifully accompanied her upstairs to their rooms and delivered her into the devoted hands of her maid before joining Little in her own bedchamber.

"Just unfasten me, if you please," Gina said. "I believe I shall sit up and read for a time and will blow the candles out myself. I expect you need your rest after a hard day in the sick room."

For the first time, she did feel guilty now. Not that she had lied *precisely* to Little, who had looked after her since she was twelve years old, but that she was misleading her. Because Little would most definitely disapprove of what she was about to do.

So would Mrs. Fitzwilliam.

So would Papa.

Well, none of them have to marry Lord Longton.

Little frowned, but merely shrugged, reminded her about dousing the candles, and went on her way.

Gina settled down to wait for quiet. The maids shared a tiny chamber between her own and Mrs. Fitzwilliam's, so she would hear Little's snoring through the wall.

How did one dress for an assignation?

So as not to be recognized. So, her traveling cloak with the hood. But she was already unlaced for bed. Stupidly, the thought made her blush, but she couldn't manage to refasten everything herself. A shawl, she decided, creeping to her open trunk and dragging one out. After a moment's pause, she wriggled until she could remove the stays from beneath her gown, and placed the garment on the chair beside her. Then she returned to her book, where the words danced incomprehensibly on the page.

The image of Rollo Darblay kept intruding. Rollo, half-foxed, smiling at her in the ladies' lounge, scowling into his drink. Rollo's eyes laughing wickedly through his mask, clouding with desire as he kissed her. Rollo's hands, Rollo's arms, Rollo's sheer fun.

Oh God, I will miss him.

Don't think of that. Think of tonight. But that made her too anxious, for she had no idea how to behave or what she would face. She might trust Rollo to manage the business, but she could not manage her own reactions.

If he makes love as he kisses, I am right to do this.

But what she had asked him for was different. Everyone kissed. Everyone didn't…

She sat up suddenly as another thought struck her. She had been brought up largely in the country. She knew what the results of physical intimacy between males and females could be. What if she conceived a baby with Rollo?

Passing another man's child off as her husband's *did* seem a betrayal, and one Longton would not have agreed to, however much money she brought him.

I should never, ever have begun this! What was I thinking of?

Rollo had said he would understand if she changed her mind. She should not go.

That decision did not make her happy either.

Through the wall, came Little's faint, muffled snores.

Time to go. Or stay.

Chapter Five

She drew in her breath, pulled the shawl tighter, and rose from the bed. For she owed Rollo at least an explanation, if not another question. She swung the cloak about her, then blew out all the candles, leaving only the bedside lamp turned down low.

The sitting room was in darkness, no light appeared under Mrs. Fitzwilliam's door or the maids'. She crept to the outer door by memory and feel, unlocked it as softly as she could, and emerged into the passage.

As on the previous nights, lights burned in wall sconces on each landing and passage, lending the darkness a somehow friendly glow. Rollo's room was on the floor above. *What if I knock on the wrong door?*

She had a nasty moment when a man passed her on the stairs, going in the other direction, but she kept her head down, and he merely mumbled an apology and kept going.

In the passage above, the door she believed to be Rollo's stood helpfully ajar. Her heart thudded as she stood outside it. Anxiety, desire, and sorrow combined to deprive her of breath and courage. Her fingers hovered an inch from the door. Then it swung open, and Rollo hauled her inside by the arm.

"Rollo, wait, wait," she hissed as he closed and locked the door behind her. "It just came to me that I can't do this. What if there is a child?"

He stood in front of her, in his shirt sleeves. Without his cravat, the strong, attractive column of his throat distracted her momentarily.

She frowned up at him, pleading, though for what she barely knew. Her hood fell back, and his gaze flitted over her hair and lips and throat and back to her eyes. In the candlelight, he seemed suddenly like a stranger, the sharp, handsome lines and planes of his face harsher, his eyes glittering.

"A child is always possible," he admitted, "but I can take steps to make it unlikely. In my favor, I've sired no children so far." He frowned, adding cautiously, "To my knowledge."

She supposed that was shocking in its way but for some reason, she wanted to laugh. He was Rollo again.

"I came to cry off," she said, "but I hoped you would have a solution."

"You scare me, Gina Wallace."

"I do?"

"I've never had an innocent in my bed before. And yet I can think of nothing but you." His arms lifted, as though he would embrace her, and then fell to his sides. "You owe me nothing. Do you want to go?"

She swallowed. Then, slowly, she shook her head.

A smile flickered over his face, and he reached up to remove her cloak, throwing it onto the nearest chair.

She glanced around his room, which was a mere bedchamber. The curtains were drawn, and enough lamps and candles were lit to provide a warm glow. Apart from the canopied bed, which she avoided looking at, there was a wardrobe, a dressing table, bedside cabinets, a desk, and a washstand. His coat was flung over the hard chair by the desk. He was not, she thought, a tidy man by nature, but he seemed to have cleared up for her visit. Or a servant had.

The room smelled of him. And he smelled...wonderful. Warmth, spice, the outdoors. And no alcohol on the breath mingling with hers. Rollo Darblay was as sober as she. Bizarrely, that was intoxicating.

"Come and sit down," he said, indicating not the bed but the sofa by the fireplace. "Would you like a glass of wine?"

While she sat, he walked to a side table where two decanters and glasses waited on a silver tray. He sloshed amber liquid into one glass and glanced back at her.

"No, thank you," she said nervously. She swallowed. "Perhaps I could have a taste of yours."

The smile flickered again. He swiped up the glass and came to sit beside her. Close but not touching. He offered her the glass, and she took it, her fingertips brushing his. Her skin tingled. She took a tiny sip, not caring much for the taste, although the shock of the burning liquid helped to settle her nerves.

"You said you would not be a polite lover," she recalled, passing back the glass. "It seems to me, you are being very polite."

"That bit comes later, but I might have used the wrong word. I hope I'll always be courteous." He drank and regarded her over the rim of the glass with glinting eyes. "But I would like us both to be naked and lost in each other. No civilized hiding—not for me at any rate."

She blushed with a sudden rush of emotion. Embarrassment? Or sheer, shocking arousal? The smile in his eyes died. His long black lashes came down, veiling his expression, and he set the glass deliberately on the table beside him.

"Gina, we don't have to do this."

In sudden terror that he would withdraw his agreement, she threw herself against him, reaching for his mouth, for another of those kisses that had made her so very certain.

Startled, he caught her in his arms, his parted lips still under hers, letting her kiss him. His lips tasted good and felt better, warm and firm. And then, as if he couldn't help it, his mouth opened wider and bore down, moving on hers with a slow, sweet sensuality she had never guessed at. His tongue swept over her lips, and she gasped, opening to him in wonder.

He drew her onto his lap and she sank against his chest, burying her hands in his hair, stroking his slightly roughened jaw and whatever part of his lips wasn't covered by her own. He caressed her back and hips, her thigh, and instead of being shocked, she sighed into his mouth.

His kisses were so drugging that she barely noticed when he plucked off her shawl. But when his fingers explored the naked skin beneath her unlaced gown and chemise, she shivered with pleasure. His kisses moved across her jaw and down her throat and shoulders, nudging aside her gown, and her hands slipped inside his shirt. She loved the hot, velvety texture of his skin, and wanted more. She plucked at his waistcoat buttons, unfastening them with urgent fingers. He helped, shrugging out of it and tossing it aside before catching his shirt and hauling it over his head in one swift motion.

She smiled, burying her mouth in his throat, before trailing kisses over his shoulders and chest. She loved the play of his muscles under her touch… He shifted her in his lap, and she felt the hard column of his erection between her thighs.

A small, inarticulate sound fell from her lips. She felt wonderful, blissful, and yet curiously hot and desperate, especially once he began to rock subtly.

"Let me make you more comfortable," he said huskily and rose with her in his arms as though she weighed nothing. Only then, with the slide of her shift did she realize she was naked save for her stockings and shoes. She kicked off the latter, and he smiled as he walked with her to the bed and laid her there.

He paused, one knee on the bed, his breathing shallow as he devoured her with glittering, predatory eyes. She made a quick, instinctive move to cover herself, but he caught her hands.

"Don't," he breathed. "You are beautiful."

And suddenly she *felt* beautiful, alluring, and powerful, just because of her effect on him. "So are you," she whispered, reaching up to run her hands over his broad, muscular shoulders.

"There's more of me," he promised, unbuttoning his pantaloons.

She was glad her first sight of a naked man was Rollo. She could not look away, for the strangeness of masculine beauty both bothered and fascinated her. He knelt on the bed, almost covering her, and kissed her mouth, while his fingers trailed down to her breast, where they circled and teased and cupped.

She arched up into him, gasping, sweeping her hands down his long back to his narrow hips and buttocks. His mouth followed his hands in a journey of utter delight until his fingers caressed her thigh and slid inward.

She let out a moan as his hand settled, understanding, at last, that *this* was the seat of her *bother*. The bliss of his caresses was sharper here, increasing both pleasure and desperation until joy swept over her so intensely that she cried out, gasping in wonder.

"So, that…" She all but panted as she began to come back to earth. "But…you did not—"

He slid inside her, and she stilled, her eyes widening. He waited a moment, his heart hammering beneath her hand, and then, when she relaxed, he said, "Again," and pushed again, filling her.

There was shock, a moment of discomfort, of strangeness, but no pain. And then he began to move, holding her gaze with his so that she could see the pleasure he took from her. In moments, she forgot everything except the slow, sensual thrust of his body, delighting hers in new, overwhelming ways.

Even in the midst of passion, he possessed his own elegance, undulating and responding to her every caress until she felt the build-up of that hot, delicious wave once more. Different this time, deeper and even more relentless.

As her body began to convulse, he groaned and suddenly everything was wild and hard and gloriously out of control. And as she fell apart around him, he reared up, all but growling. Dear God, he was magnificent… He pulled himself from her body and collapsed upon her, his open mouth finding her in a gasping, devouring kiss.

Awed, she held on to him tightly. And smiled, because he had given her such stunning pleasure and received it.

>>><<<

Rollo had lost a bit of his determined control just at the end. Her delight in his caresses, her bewildered joy in the pleasures he had shown her had both touched and pleased him. But when she had clung to him, matching his every move with uninhibited fervor, she had taken him by surprise. He had fallen into the blind intensity of passion and forgotten some of the care and courtesy he had promised them both. He had almost failed to withdraw, although thank God he'd retained enough sense to manage it just in time. And even so, the *pleasure*…

God, she was amazing. And sweet and passionate and lovely. And he had behaved like a beast.

When his heart was calm enough to move, he eased his weight off her to stare down into her face. She was smiling.

Surprised, he said urgently, "Did I hurt you?"

"No. I had no idea, I never guessed it was so…"

He settled beside her, gathering her close in his arms. "Neither did I. You are an utter delight."

She rearranged her arms around him, burying her face in his shoulder. "Thank you," she said in a muffled voice. "Thank you for giving me this."

"Darling, it's I who thank you."

Something wetter than the faint sheen of sweat spread on his shoulder. A faint shudder passed through her.

"Gina? Are you crying? I didn't mean to make you cry." Helplessly, he stroked her hair and kissed the top of her head.

"I'm just happy," she said huskily. There was a pause. Then, incurably honest, she added, "And a little sad because this is all I will ever have with you."

Rollo listened to the beat of his heart, to the rhythm of her breathing as the plan he had already rejected forced its way back up. It seemed more imperative now.

"It needn't be," he said.

Her arm tightened around him. "I can't," she whispered. "I can't be that kind of wife. Even for you."

"Then change husbands. If your father wants a noble fortune hunter, have me instead."

She raised her head to stare at him.

"Why not? We would have fun, being married, don't you think?"

Her eyes gleamed as she thought about it, and he held his breath, willing her to see the possibilities, especially in the light of what they had just given each other. It was, truly, the perfect solution for both of them. He could see the rise of hope, of excitement glowing in her beautiful eyes.

And then they turned bleak.

"You are a viscount," she said tragically. "Longton is an earl, to whom my father gave his word. I know you would never regard him as a gentleman, but it is a point of honor with my father that he *never* breaks his word."

"You never gave yours," he pointed out.

She closed her eyes. "Don't, Rollo. Please, don't."

When he thought she might bolt from the bed, she flung herself over him and kissed him. "Thank you for that, too. I will treasure it. You will never know how much."

Rollo could recognize a lost cause when he came upon one. And he was not a man used to wasting much time on such. He tried and, if he failed, he moved on, usually further down the road to the devil. But now, he knew a powerful urge to save Gina, to persuade her, to spill out Longton's reputation with the ton, his character, and his excesses. He was no fit husband for her.

But then, God knew, neither was Rollo. If someone had spilled out *his* reputation, character, and excesses into Gina's ear before tonight, he very much doubted he would be here. The girl had the right to choose her own doom, and at least Longton would die before Rollo and leave her in peace.

His arms tightened around her involuntarily. "If you change your mind," he whispered in her ear. "Just say the word." It was all he could do. Give her a Hobson's choice. One bad bargain or another. And he knew she would always take her father's choice because she would not break his word.

"Oh, Rollo," she whispered back. "You have to marry, too."

He did, though he refused to think about that in bed with Gina. "Not until you do." He took a breath. "When will you be sure you haven't conceived?"

She drew back again, gazing at him in bewilderment. And then, even in the pale light, he could see her blush to the roots of her hair. "A few days."

"Then you must promise to tell me if you have," he said. "You *must* marry me then, for I'll not have a child of mine brought up by Longton."

Although she remained close, some of the happiness in her eyes died. "Is he as bad as that?"

"He's not pretty," Rollo admitted. "But then, neither am I." He stroked her hair and rolled her beneath him to kiss her back to happiness. "I swear I would do right by you, by our child."

Inevitably, as she clung to him, arousal grew again. He ignored it, from consideration for her, and in time, he fell into a contented sleep with Gina cradled in his arms.

WHEN HE WOKE, his arms were empty and she had gone. He felt ridiculously hurt by that, for losing some of the only precious time they would have together. How could he have fallen asleep? She clearly hadn't, or not for long.

But he could not have kept her here until morning. She would have been seen leaving his room or returning to her own. *Perhaps then, she would have married me.*

Appalled by the wistful note of the thought, he scowled. *And perhaps not. She has chosen her doom, and now I have to be man enough to face mine.*

He would take his courage from hers, get the damned thing over with.

Rising, he rang for coffee and toast and washed and dressed quickly. He was adept without a valet, never having had one except a part share in his father's when he came home from Oxford.

He drank his coffee and ate his toast gazing out of the window. An old-fashioned traveling coach was being loaded up with trunks and bags, supervised by two ladies' maids. On impulse, as he did most things, Rollo dropped his toast and bolted across the room to the door, along the passage, and down the staircase to the foyer. Here, sense overtook him enough that he did not bolt outside and throw himself before Miss Wallace just to force her to see him.

Instead, he moved briskly as though heading out for his morning walk, just as he had done yesterday. He even exchanged a word with the porter, though he had no idea what either of them said. Outside, an elegant middle-aged lady in puce was being handed into the traveling coach. She looked vaguely familiar. Waiting by the door was a younger woman whose profile he recognized only too well.

Would she be angry that he was there? Embarrassed? Would she even see him?

She turned her head and warmth filled her eyes. A smile curved her lips, a smile of loss and friendship and gratitude. His throat closed up. For the first time in years, he wanted to weep. He didn't. He inclined his head in a slight bow, as one might give a stranger, and smiled back just because she was wonderful.

Then she turned away, the servant handed her into the carriage, and Rollo walked off.

Chapter Six

On Wednesday morning, Gina woke to the knowledge that she had not conceived a child with Rollo Darblay. Although this considerably simplified her life, she wept into her pillow for several minutes before she wiped her eyes and rose to deal with the day.

This began with a trip to the dressmaker, for Mrs. Fitzwilliam, having inspected her wardrobe, had pronounced that she did not have nearly enough gowns to last for two weeks in town, let alone for a month or more.

"I have five morning dresses, a riding habit, five evening gowns, and two ballgowns," Gina had pointed out. "How is that not enough?"

"My dear, this is London. You cannot be seen wearing the same gown twice. At least not in the evenings, and probably not at Venetian breakfasts either. At least what you do have will not be spotted as provincial, for they are well made, and you do have excellent taste."

Gina had given in, although London prices were mind-bogglingly higher than Manchester. Today, she was to have a fitting for the new evening gowns, and Mrs. Fitzwilliam had persuaded her of her need for a second riding habit, new walking dresses, and various sundries such as new hats, gloves, reticules, and dancing slippers. And an opera cloak.

Gina's Puritan soul was appalled, although she did find the acquisition of beautiful new clothes as entertaining as most did. They had spent the last two days leaving cards at the homes of Mrs. Fitzwilliam's acquaintances, and yesterday, they had received a few very fashionable morning callers, along with Lord Longton, whose eyes had gleamed approval at the sight of her.

To her relief, his lordship had attempted no lover-like gestures. She would need to get considerably more used to him before she could tolerate such advances. In fact, he had merely stayed the requisite half an hour and toddled off again.

Gina found Mrs. Fitzwilliam in the breakfast parlor, happily sorting through the morning's post.

"Ah, there you are, Gina! Invitations are trickling in from the best people, and after this evening, I will expect a flood."

"Why, what happens this evening?" Gina asked, loading her plate with eggs, ham, and a morsel of smoked fish.

"The opera!" Mrs. Fitzwilliam exclaimed. "Everyone will be there!"

Except for Lord Darblay, who couldn't bear the screeching. The thought made her smile, even as she wondered what it would be like to meet him again. Would they still be friends? Would he ignore her? Flirt with her? Forget her?

She should certainly forget him, but her little plan of a stolen night of love to ease her ensuing life of duty was not bearing up well in her mind. Although she tried to concentrate on the present, she kept remembering some saying, some expression, or amusing moment she and Rollo had shared. She would find herself dwelling on their dances, kisses, and the ecstasy of her body that he had unlocked.

It was not so easy to move on. But then, it had only been a few days.

"Of course," Gina said meekly.

"Then tomorrow, we have a Venetian breakfast at Mrs. Farrow's, and Lady Rampton's soiree in the evening. Lord Longton will be there, if you recall.

"I do." And it would be all to the good to get to meet him. Really, it would. She could not marry a stranger.

"I'm afraid all my friends are a little old and stuffy," Mrs. Fitzwilliam said apologetically, "but you will soon make your own friends among the younger set and be asked everywhere."

"Despite my birth?"

"My dear, it will soon be forgotten in the respectability of *my* birth and your fortune."

Which was mind-bogglingly honest, if nothing else.

The day duly passed in a welter of shopping, calls, and walking in the park. During the daily gathering in Hyde Park—"Everyone goes to be seen," Mrs. Fitzwilliam assured her—she had the pleasure of observing the ton. Among the fashionable, the beautiful, and the fribbles, Gina most enjoyed the few eccentrics—the dashing lady who drove herself so skillfully in a high-perch phaeton, the gentleman in outrageous costume with a red handkerchief knotted about his throat instead of a cravat.

"Poet," Mrs. Fitzwilliam commented, seeing the direction of her gaze. "He's young and will grow out of it."

"Oh, and ma'am, who is that?"

Another lady driving herself had caught Gina's attention, but this woman was much more noticeable. Older and considerably plumper, dressed in shades of orange and purple, she genuinely startled the eye. Many people looked, but no one she passed seemed to see her, and where the younger lady driving herself had paused often to talk to acquaintances, even to take up a favored passenger for a turn, the lady in orange stopped for no one.

Mrs. Fitzwilliam sniffed. "That is Mrs. Snodgrass, reported to be the richest widow in London. From trade, you understand. She is not one of us, and you will not meet her."

Gina cast her a sardonic glance. "*I* am not one of you."

"By an accident of birth," Mrs. Fitzwilliam said with dignity. "*You* are not vulgar."

"She must be quite brave," Gina said thoughtfully.

"Or thick-skinned."

Despite Mrs. Fitzwilliam's assurance, the bold, despised woman stuck in Gina's mind. She was conscious of a fellow feeling for her. Mrs. Snodgrass had not, like Gina, a friend of the ton to guide her and lend her the trappings of acceptability. But even so, the woman was a reminder that Gina herself would never be accepted either, only tolerated with a veil of politeness.

She could imagine the whispers. *"Poor old Longton, nothing for it but to marry so low for the money."*

But it was the life her father wanted for his children and grandchildren, and Gina was the means.

Mrs. Fitzwilliam's cheerful young nephew, Mr. Godfrey Fitzwilliam—"call me Fitz!"—joined them for dinner in the evening, since he was to be their escort to the opera. Although he greeted Gina with perfect courtesy, she caught him observing her more than once, as though surprised she didn't slurp her soup or eat her meat off the knife. However, once he relaxed, he proved himself entertaining company and was a very pleasant escort to Covent Garden.

At first, an evening at the opera seemed to be exactly the same exercise as walking or driving in Hyde Park at five of the clock. Mrs. Fitzwilliam scoured the other boxes, smiling and nodding to acquaintances, even chatting to the lady in the neighboring box. The noise was phenomenal, the various expensive perfumes of the patrons combined in the heat of the candles in a dizzying, headache-threatening kind of way.

Gina tried to focus on something, forcing herself to count the boxes in the same row as her own, until she came to one containing the colorful figure of Mrs. Snodgrass, the wealthy cit's widow. This evening, she wore jonquil trimmed with deep blue, and a spectacular, jeweled turban. It was difficult to look away, and Gina could not help noticing that she was not alone. An almost invisible woman sat beside her, and two gentlemen appeared to be paying court to her.

"You're dazzled by Mrs. Snodgrass?" Mr. Fitzwilliam murmured. "Aren't we all?"

"The gentlemen with her appear to be."

"Word is they'll have to work hard before Darblay cuts in."

The name hit her in the chest like a blow, making her ears sing. "Darblay?" she managed.

"The new viscount, Rollo. Friend of mine, actually. Best of good fellows, but finds himself in straitened circumstances, if you know what I mean."

Yes, I know exactly what you mean. Rollo's words on the subject of his prospective marriage partners came back to her. *"Miss Gush and Mrs. Take-me-as-I-am… One is a trifle long in the tooth, and the other some screeching schoolgirl."* Gina felt sad for Mrs. Snodgrass all over again. And for him.

Mr. Fitzwilliam, who knew of her connection to Lord Longton, seemed to realize the too-close associations of what he had just said, for he looked appalled and broke into hurried speech once more. "Of course, she'll be doing him a favor. The careful mamas all warn their daughters against Rolls."

"Because of his character or his poverty?" Gina asked sardonically.

"Both, I should think."

They were both saved further conversation by the rise of the stage curtain and a very pretty display of dancing. Not that anyone else seemed to see the need to stop talking. If anything, the hum rose in order to be heard over the music.

The first interval brought a stream of visitors to their box, and so many introductions that Gina had no hope of remembering them. Many were debutantes with their proud mamas or young matrons, and Mrs. Fitzwilliam was proved right that she did form the beginnings of several friendships. Gina wondered cynically if their warmth would outlast the revelation of her birth. But for the moment, at least, Mrs. Fitzwilliam's respectability provided a cloak of protection.

At the second interval, Mrs. Fitzwilliam issued fresh instructions. "Godfrey, take Miss Wallace to visit your own friends—

only the respectable ones, mind!—and be back before the second act."

Obediently, they left her to pass along the milling corridor.

"At least it is cooler out here," Gina said in some relief. "The singing is lovely, but the heat is becoming overwhelming."

"We can just stroll around if you like. To be honest, most of the fellows I know are in the pit. Oh, there's Holles, of course. Bit serious but amiable and already engaged to be married to a very sweet lady. We could drop in on them if you like."

"If you think they would not mind."

"They'll be charmed," he assured her, guiding her to the stairs.

"Evening, Fitz," a good-looking young man greeted him in some surprise when they entered the box at last. "Opera's not your usual fare, is it?"

"Nor yours," Fitz retorted.

"True. You're acquainted with Mrs. Dove, aren't you? And Miss Dove, my betrothed?"

"Of course! How do you do, ma'am? Miss Dove?" He exchanged amiable bows with both ladies and presented Gina as his aunt's protegee, before introducing her to Mr. Holles.

"So, you have just arrived in town?" Miss Dove said as Gina sat down beside her. "Do you find it completely overwhelming? I know I did."

"There are so many *people*," Gina blurted.

"I know. And even the ones you're introduced to, you can't remember their names! And there is no peace. Apart from the park."

"Hyde Park? It does not seem so very peaceful to me."

"Oh, it is in the morning. We usually take our dog for an early walk. You should join us sometime."

"Thank you, I should like to. Would I need to bring my maid?"

Miss Dove frowned. "Perhaps. We never do, but then we have Pup, who is quite the scariest chaperone ever to grace the park. If you're staying with Mrs. Fitzwilliam, I'll send you a note one morning, shall I?"

"Yes, please do."

Other people entered the box then, and she and Fitz left to make room. As they made their way along the corridor, she saw the unmistakable figure of Mrs. Snodgrass sailing in the opposite direction. She appeared to be in a hurry, wafting her fan almost dementedly. She stumbled and flung out one hand to the wall to stop herself from falling, and her reticule fell to the floor, spilling some of its contents.

To Gina's amazement, a gentleman stepped over the items and kept walking, although he had to have seen. Without thought, Gina stepped closer and crouched down, gathering the fallen comb and coin purse back into the reticule. She rose and held it out to the lady, who looked both surprised and touched.

"Bless you, my dear, there was no need for that."

"Well, I'm quicker on my feet than Mr. Fitzwilliam," Gina said, knowing that beside her Fitz was blushing scarlet.

"Certainly quicker than me," said Mrs. Snodgrass with a jolly laugh. "I'm too plump to bend these days!"

She may have been, but up close, she was also younger than Gina had originally thought. She was in her thirties rather than her forties, and her smile was actually quite pretty.

"Thank you," Mrs. Snodgrass said and moved on.

Fitz all but dragged Gina in the opposite direction. "Sorry, I should have done that, not you."

"Yes, you should," Gina agreed. "But that man who simply stepped over the top was just plain rude." It should have been some comfort that Rollo Darblay, whatever was said about him, would never be so ungentlemanly toward her.

ROLLO DARBLAY, MEANTIME, had been conscientiously reviewing

his options. He would do nothing, of course, until he knew there had been no consequences to his encounter with Gina Wallace. But, encouraged by her bravery and by the morose sight of his mother drifting about the townhouse in deepest black, he paid a call on each of his potential brides.

He began with Miss Smythe, who was thrown into raptures by his arrival. She was just eighteen years old, and her undeniable beauty had raised her parents' ambitions to the nobility. When Rollo had first seen her, she had reminded him of a slightly younger version of Maddy, his favorite ladybird, and it was for that reason he had imagined he might tolerate marriage to her.

She certainly greeted him with enthusiasm, jumping up from her chair and exclaiming, "My lord!" She hurried across the floor, hands held out to him before even her mother could get near him. "We had quite given you up!"

He took her hands and bowed over them. "I was out of town," he said by way of explanation, although he owed her none. They had met only twice.

"Besides, his lordship is in mourning," her mother scolded. "He can't go dashing off to parties just to dance with you." She curtseyed, which at least gave him an excuse to extract his hands from her daughter's and bow.

But almost immediately, Miss Smythe grasped his arm, hugging it to her while she nearly danced across the room to the sofa, ejecting its current, affronted occupant with an imperious flick of her fingers.

Under this swain's scowl, Rollo sought to hand her civilly onto one side of the sofa, but like a limpet, she clung to his arm, all but dragging him down with her. Rollo, who had no desire for tea, happily accepted a cup, just to free himself from her physical clutches. While he drank, she chattered away about what entertainments she had been to over the last few days and what lay in store.

Rollo felt his mind glaze over. In search of some occupation for it, he gazed around the room. Mrs. Smythe, proudly beamed upon them both, and the three angry young men, presumably Miss Smythe's suitors, all glared at Rollo. Inappropriately, he felt his lips twitch and coughed to prevent the laughter from escaping.

He left after one cup of tea and, striding up the street, he felt rather like dusting himself off. Next, for comparison purposes, he knocked on the door of Mrs. Snodgrass's large townhouse on the edges of Mayfair.

The butler showed him to the drawing room, which contained only two women. On one chair, the little dab of a female whose name he could not remember was plying needlework. Mrs. Snodgrass herself, resplendent in purple and orange, sat at a spindly-legged bureau, busily writing, though she stood when he was announced and walked forward to meet him.

"A pleasant surprise, my lord," she said briskly. "A cup of tea, perhaps?"

"God, no," Rollo said involuntarily, then at the gleam of laughter in his hostess's eyes, he grinned. "Sorry. Don't mean to be rude. I've just swilled enough to last me for a week."

She indicated a chair, and he bowed to the other lady before sitting on the other end of the sofa from Mrs. Snodgrass. Fortunately, she seemed to feel no urge to clutch him.

"In that case, what can we do for you?" Mrs. Snodgrass asked briskly.

"Nothing," Rollo replied. "Just paying a call to see how you go on."

"Life in mourning is that dull?"

"Well, it is dull," he agreed, "though worse for my sister. Beats me why women are expected to mourn more than men."

"Because they have nothing else to do with their time, of course."

"Hmm," he said skeptically, glancing at her desk which was heaped with papers. "Anyway, the point is, of course, I didn't call from boredom."

"Perhaps you came to invite me to the opera?"

He shuddered. "Anything but that, ma'am. Happy to take you driving in the park if you can spare the time?"

"I prefer to drive myself," she said bluntly. Rollo rather liked that about her. "I suppose mourning means you don't attend balls."

Apart from Maida. *Don't think about that.* "Well, not to dance," he said dubiously. "Though to be honest, I'm making it up as I go on. Never been in mourning before, and I'm not really one to follow the rules in any case."

"No, I like that about you," Mrs. Snodgrass said. She tapped one finger against her lips. "I suppose you might drop in at Lady Rampton's soiree tomorrow evening?"

"I might," he said dubiously. "She sent me a card, probably because I went once before. Horrible affair, I assure you. Fellows spouting poetry, and some screeching soprano—"

"I like poetry," Mrs. Snodgrass interrupted.

"Do you? Well, if you mean to be there, I might make the effort."

"Sadly," she said, examining her fingernails, "I have not been invited." She glanced up and met his gaze.

Rollo's lips twitched. "You want me to take you? Judging Lady Rampton won't cause a scene by refusing you entry if you're on my arm?"

Mrs. Snodgrass smiled, and Rollo gave a crack of laughter. "I'll do it."

"You're doing *what*?" his friend Montague demanded an hour later. He and Meade had turned up at Darblay House to keep Rollo company and entice him out for a quiet dinner at the club and were sprawled comfortably in Rollo's dressing room.

"Taking Mrs. Snodgrass to the Ramptons' soiree."

Meade gave a snort of laughter. "I see what you're up to.

Lady Rampton would never invite someone of such bad ton. You're daring her to throw Mrs. Snoddy out. And I must admit, I'd love to see her ladyship's face when you turn up with Mrs. S. on your arm! You're evil, Rolls."

"I like Mrs. S."

His friends exchanged glances.

Montague took out a flask and passed it to Rollo. "Does this mean you've made up your mind to marry her?"

"Thinking about it," Rollo said bleakly. He took a swig from the flask and passed it to Meade.

"She'd certainly solve all your financial worries in one fell swoop," Meade allowed. "Not sure she's the kind to hand over the reins, as it were."

"True," Rollo agreed. "There would be some mean settlements in place to stop me plowing through her entire fortune. Not unreasonable if the debts are gone and the money's spent on the estate."

"But would it be?" Montague asked. "She might prove to be the same obstacle as your father—God rest him."

"I don't think it would be an issue." Rollo accepted the flask once more, but since it was empty, he passed it back to Montague. "And frankly, if it's a question of her or putting up with the fawning and screeching of Miss Smythe, I'd pick Mrs. Snoddy any day of the week. At least she makes me laugh."

With the words, another laughing face swam into his mind. But he would not think of Gina Wallace. Not until after tomorrow, when she would have more idea if they had conceived a child. He had already discovered where she was, and it was a bit of luck that he knew Fitz, her chaperone's nephew.

It was certainly amusing to escort Mrs. Snodgrass to Lady Rampton's, although when he called for her, he was almost disappointed she had toned down her outrageous color combinations. Instead, she wore an ornate gown of fashionable Pomona silk, with a matching turban. Diamonds dripped from her neck and ears, wrists, and fingers. In her own way, she looked rather magnificent, but Lady Rampton would still be outraged.

"Sure you want to put yourself through this?" Rollo asked. "Happy to take you to the theatre instead, or anywhere else you'd like to go."

"Lady Rampton's will do nicely. Unless your lordship is getting cold feet?"

Rollo grinned. "Not I, Mrs. S. Shall we go?"

CHAPTER SEVEN

FITZ HAD BEEN reluctantly dragooned into escorting his aunt and Gina to Lady Rampton's soiree. "Not my usual thing," he had pleaded. "And Lady Rampton scares me to death."

"Nonsense," his aunt said briskly. "It is good to widen your horizons occasionally, and as for Lady Rampton, she's just a bit high in the instep. She has no reason to look down her nose at you."

"I know that, but whenever she does look at me, I'm sure she knows about that jam I stole from the kitchen and ate in bed with a spoon."

Gina laughed. "How old were you?"

"Five," he admitted.

Unsurprisingly, his aunt dismissed this as nonsense, and he duly accompanied them to the salons of Sedgemoor House. They were welcomed at the door by Lady Rampton—a very regal matron, who appeared older than her years—accompanied by her husband and her father-in-law, the Marquess of Sedgemoor.

Her ladyship, on being introduced to Gina, condescended to a gracious smile. "How pretty you are, my dear."

"Thank you, my lady," was all Gina could think of to reply, though her ladyship's attention was now on Fitz, bowing over her hand.

"Made it," he murmured a moment later, following his aunt

and Gina into the room. "Let's find a seat for you and a glass of... Good Lord! What the devil are *they* doing here?" He grinned as two young men ambled over to them. They were maybe a couple of years older than Fitz but bore the same air of discomfort as he in such surroundings. "Aunt, are you acquainted with Mr. Meade and Mr. Montague? Friends of mine! Gentlemen, my aunt, Mrs. Fitzwilliam. And this is her protegee, Miss Wallace."

Both gentlemen bowed correctly and pronounced themselves charmed. Mr. Meade offered to fetch wine or lemonade for the ladies, which Mrs. Fitzwilliam graciously accepted.

Gina looked about her. A throng of fashionable people were scattered about a large room, where a very fine pianoforte had been given pride of place. Some were milling in and out of a doorway at the far end.

"I wouldn't go there," Mr. Montague confided, seeing the direction of her gaze. "Some quiz in lace is reciting *poetry*."

Gina smiled sympathetically, though Mrs. Fitzwilliam said, "Are you sure you are at the right party, Mr. Montague? Music, poetry, and the arts are the whole point of such evenings."

Fitz grinned at his friend's hunted expression. "Why *did* you come?"

"To own the truth, just because—"

"Ladies," interrupted an older voice that made Gina's heart sink with a thud. However, she managed to keep the smile on her lips as she turned to offer her hand to Lord Longton, who bowed over it. "I am more than usually thrilled to see you since you have preserved me from a discussion about Horace. I confess to barely remembering a word of the fellow when I left Oxford, so truly, what can I contribute now?"

"Then what you made join such a discussion, my lord?" Gina asked with genuine curiosity.

"I knew the fellow who is prosing on. And I arrived early, so it was a choice between that and the poetry."

Fitz and Mr. Montague nodded sympathetically.

"Why do you all come to such gatherings?" Gina blurted.

"For the music, Miss Wallace," his lordship said blandly, taking the glass Mr. Meade was about to present to her, and offering it to her himself. "I hear the pianist is quite out of the ordinary. And, of course, I hoped for the felicity of your presence. Where may I escort you? In the other room, there is a small exhibition of portraits by young Mr. Dornan which might interest you. Although you will have to put up with the poetry in the far corner."

At that moment, a ripple of disturbance swept around the room. Talk died away as all eyes turned toward the salon door, where Lady Rampton was greeting her newest guests. The air seemed to fly from Gina's lungs. This time, her heart did not sink, but lurched once with a thud she feared was audible, and then beat a quick, merciless tattoo.

Rollo, Viscount Darblay, had entered the room.

In truth, he swaggered in with familiar, careless elegance, as though quite unaware of the stir he caused, largely because of the lady on his arm. Mrs. Snodgrass, splendid in layers and flounces of Pomona silk and diamonds.

"That's why," Mr. Montague whispered to Fitz, and both he and Mr. Meade detached themselves. Meade went immediately forward to greet the couple, while Montague collected wine. And thus was Mrs. Snodgrass saved from being ignored and isolated as soon as she stepped into the room.

Behind them, Lady Rampton was trying to look as though she were not appalled and entirely unable to deal with the situation.

"What a complete hand he is," Fitz said with a grin.

And he was. But somehow Gina could not quite appreciate it. She could not admire and laugh at his bold impudence, for the fact that he had brought her surely meant that Mrs. Snodgrass had indeed been his *"Mrs. Take-me-as-you-find-me, long-in-the-tooth"* marriage option, and that he had made his decision. He would marry Mrs. Snodgrass.

Why could she not smile and wish him well? She stood beside

the man she would marry for reasons quite as calculating. Yet she already missed Rollo with intense sweet sadness that she was trying to use to bolster her strength. But never had she imagined that his marriage would hit her with such a blow that she reeled from the sheer hurt.

And then, as his gaze swept around the room, it landed on hers and held.

From close by came outraged whispers of the gossips, like the annoying buzz of flies. "My dear, what *is* he about to bring such a creature here?"

"Well, the Darblays are quite rolled up you know. Nothing else for it but to marry money. Poor fellow."

"But need she quite so…vulgar?"

"Goes with the money, my dear, but goodness, poor Lady Darblay. Can you imagine?"

Her gaze trapped by Rollo's, Gina watched his reckless smile grow fixed. He took one, probably involuntary step toward her, and with that Mrs. Snodgrass sailed forward, too, obliging Rollo to accompany her.

"Quick, hide!" Mrs. Fitzwilliam hissed.

In other circumstances, Gina would have found that exquisitely funny, for short of bolting, there was nowhere to hide. And Mrs. Fitzwilliam was not capable of that degree of rudeness.

Rollo, of course, carried it off with nonchalant grace. "Good evening, Mrs. Fitzwilliam. My lord. Fitz. Allow me to present Mrs. Snodgrass. Ma'am, Mrs. Fitzwilliam."

Mrs. Fitzwilliam inclined her head as graciously as she could, and Mrs. Snodgrass's eyes moved on to Gina and smiled.

"Why, we have met, have we not?"

"You have?" Mrs. Fitzwilliam said faintly.

"At the opera," Mrs. Snodgrass said, "when I was so clumsy as to drop everything."

"A mere accident, ma'am." Since Gina was afraid her chaperone simply would not introduce them, she held out her hand. "Gina Wallace."

"My protegee, Miss Wallace," Mrs. Fitzwilliam said faintly. "Lord Darblay, my dear."

Rollo bowed again, though she did not dare offer her hand, and he didn't appear to expect it, since he turned almost immediately to introduce Mrs. Snodgrass to Lord Longton. Who looked thoroughly amused by the whole thing, although he greeted the lady affably before turning to Gina. "Shall we go and look at these paintings, then?"

"Of course." She took his proffered arm, and with a quick smile for the company in general, walked across the room with him.

Her knees felt none too steady, and she thought he might have felt the faint trembling of her fingers on his arm, for he said not unkindly, "This must all be new and a bit overwhelming for you."

"I am used to knowing everyone at parties," she managed.

"Did you know Mrs. Snodgrass?"

"Not until she dropped her reticule at the opera, and even then, not by name. Why? Do you imagine all we folk in trade must be acquainted?" She spoke in jest and without thought, then glanced at him surreptitiously to see if he minded.

He was regarding her more closely than usual. "Was that a set-down, Miss Wallace?"

"Of course not," she said hastily.

He nodded graciously to acquaintances as they made their stately way into the next room. "You need not mention your father is in trade," he murmured. "Though everyone will know, no one will mention it if you do not. You may rest assured that I would not have offered for you had I not admired your ladylike behavior."

"Was that a compliment?" she asked before she could help it.

He smiled amiably. "I believe it was. Ah, here are the portraits. Who do you recognize among them?"

ROLLO WAS FURIOUS because she walked away without even looking at him.

Her presence had taken him completely by surprise, for, stupidly, it had never entered his head he might run into her here. Affairs like this were by their nature smaller and more confined than, for example, grand balls. His plan had been to call on her tomorrow, with the aid of Fitz. At least Fitz was here, a helpful reminder of why Gina's chaperone had looked familiar to him at Renwick's.

It was small comfort that she had been as surprised by him— or by his escorting Mrs. Snodgrass. There was no way to tell, and it didn't damned well matter, for she would marry the old goat her father had bought for her, and Rollo would sell himself to Mrs. Snoddy.

Until he had seen Gina again, he had thought he could do it, too, for Mrs. Snodgrass was at least jolly and clever, an outspoken woman of character, and in her own distinctive way, not unattractive. But Gina…

Gina would marry Longton. And now that he had seen them together, he felt sick.

"Is he some relation to her?" Mrs. Snodgrass asked as they strolled almost in the wake of Gina and Longton.

Rollo tried to hide his savagery. "Family friend, I believe." He swallowed, adding casually, "You met her at the opera?"

"Not exactly *met*. I'd walked along the corridor to take the air—just by myself, you understand, or there seemed no point— only then the interval took me by surprise, and hordes of people seemed to be charging at me. I was already dizzy enough. I stumbled and dropped my reticule, and all those so-called gentlemen would have walked right past. At least one did. Then that young lady left her escort and picked everything up for me. I blessed her, for if I'd had to do it, I'd have fallen over, and all those fine gentlemen would have walked over *me* instead."

So, she wasn't quite as thick-skinned as she pretended. That distracted him for a moment from Gina's innate kindness. As did the import of her words.

"You should not be that overcome, ma'am. Have you seen a physician?"

"Why would I want a quack to tell me what I already know? I'm too fat."

He could have denied it. He could have flattered her with platitudes that she would neither believe nor thank him for. "So, what are you going to do about it?"

Her eyes widened and blinked. Then she laughed, a pure, hearty sound that drew several disapproving gazes. She tucked his arm closer. "You might just be good for me, Darblay. You just might."

He should have been pleased to be making such headway in his suit, but in truth, he could not think of anything or anyone until he had spoken to Gina. And that did not prove easy. She was constantly protected by either Longton or Mrs. Fitzwilliam, hemmed in by those listening to poetry or admiring the pianist who was Lady Rampton's main attraction of the evening. Besides which, having brought Mrs. Snodgrass here, he felt compelled not to abandon her to either the wolves or isolation.

He had hoped to sit beside Gina, or at least behind her, during the pianoforte recital, but Lord Calton beat him to it, and he could hardly talk over him.

In the end, his moment came unexpectedly, after Mrs. Snodgrass had excused herself to him. While he prowled toward the supper room, he caught sight of Gina alone, hurrying across the hall toward the salon. He slipped out and strolled toward the stairs. Then, as if he had just caught sight of her, he changed direction to intercept her.

She saw him coming and paused. A faint, shy smile flickered across her face, although she still seemed poised for flight.

Rollo bowed. "Miss Wallace. Allow me to escort you back to

Mrs. Fitzwilliam."

"Thank you," she said nervously, though she took his arm.

Even that light, gloved touch brought intimate memory flooding back. *This is insufferable!*

He walked only a few steps and paused between the salon door and that to the supper room, where they could not be seen, before whisking her behind the Grecian style pillar.

"How are you?" he demanded, more brusquely than he had intended, but she didn't appear to mind.

"Well. As I see, are you."

He searched her eyes. "Then there were no consequences to our…meeting?"

"Oh, no. No one heard me return. They were all still fast asleep."

"Gina!" he said in frustration, and at last she understood for she flushed to the roots of her hair.

"Oh. That. No. No consequences."

He was conscious of a stupid, oddly sharp stab of disappointment. There was no reason to marry her. No reason why he shouldn't marry the wealthy widow, or Gina, Lord Longton.

"Thank you for asking me," she said low. "It means much to me."

Not enough. "Will you really marry him?"

"You know I must." She swallowed. "I rather like your Mrs. Snodgrass."

"Yes, so do I," he admitted. Then he scowled. "Do you like Longton?"

"Perhaps I am beginning to," she said cautiously. She was peering up at him, a faint frown of anxiety marring her brow. "Rollo, we *are* still friends?"

Voices sounded close by, women heading for the stairs. Rollo eased Gina around the pillar.

"If I can bear it," he muttered. Before he could stop himself, he snatched her hand up, peeled back her glove, and pressed his lips to her wrist. Her elusive, flowered scent, the taste of her skin, filled his senses. And beneath his mouth, her pulse galloped.

"Rollo?" she whispered, but he could not linger. Despite her gasp, he dragged her hand back to his arm and walked her smartly toward the supper room door.

Conflicting relief, loss, and desire bombarded him, but he restored her to her chaperone with no more than a careless bow before he strode off in search of the brandy.

"For your own sake, don't be encouraging Rollo Darblay," Mrs. Fitzwilliam said severely in the carriage going home. "Lord Longton won't like it, and neither will I. Nor your father."

"Rolls is not so bad." Fitz clearly felt compelled to defend his friend. "Bit of a loose screw, but he doesn't pursue respectable girls."

"Godfrey," his aunt scolded.

"Sorry, Aunt." He subsided against the opposite cushions.

"But I thought on the whole that went rather well." Mrs. Fitzwilliam beamed at Gina. "Lord Longton was most attentive, which staves off the other fortune hunters, and you were clearly accepted and well-liked. Just the thing to secure you partners for tomorrow's ball."

Gina smiled, trying to be grateful. She suspected she only wanted to dance with Lord Darblay, whose kiss still burned beneath her glove. And that would not do at all.

Chapter Eight

It was very odd, but Gina greeted the new morning with excitement, something that hadn't happened for a long time. Apart from one morning in Renwick's Hotel, but she wouldn't think of that. Instead, she thought about encountering Rollo again. After all, they had made their agreement. They would not be lovers, but they would be friends. And Rollo's friendship both supported and cheered her.

She joined Mrs. Fitzwilliam for breakfast with a cheerful, "Good morning, ma'am!"

"Good morning, my dear." Mrs. Fitzwilliam returned the greeting with a little less enthusiasm—she was not a morning person—though she did rouse herself to say, "You must rest for part of today in order to be at your best for the Carrington's ball this evening. Oh, and a note was hand-delivered for you a few minutes ago."

The note lay by her place setting, small and intriguing, but she forced herself to pile eggs and toast on her plate before walking to the table, her heart thumping. Could it be from Rollo? Would he be so indiscreet? He had kissed her hand, but that was really a respectful kiss a friend could not object to.

No, she reminded herself. *He kissed my wrist.* Which, though only a few inches away, was somehow much more intimate. He had even pulled down her glove to do it. What did…?

She unfolded the note to distract herself—it wasn't sealed—and read the signature first. *Catherine Dove.*

It was as well, though that didn't help the pang of disappointment. Miss Dove was suggesting a morning walk in the park, though she warned Miss Wallace her siblings would be present, along with their large but friendly dog.

In truth, the normal, family walk sounded just what she needed. "May I go alone, Mrs. Fitz?" she asked, passing her chaperone the note.

"The Doves are unexceptionable," Mrs. Fitzwilliam pronounced. "Eccentric but unexceptionable. Connected to the Earl of Wenning, you know, and by marriage to the Marquess of Sedgemoor. And so, to Lady Rampton, in fact. Take Little, and if you don't want the carriage, I'll send a footman with you to the gate."

Although the expedition now seemed top-heavy with servants, Gina thrust aside her spurt of irritation and prepared to enjoy a brisk walk in the nearest thing London possessed to the countryside.

Trailed by Little and George the footman, she reached the Cumberland gate to the park to discover a laughing family and a massive dog with a bark like a bear's.

"Oh, there you are, Miss Wallace," Catherine smiled, while a lad of about sixteen commanded the huge hound to sit. To Gina's surprise, it did, although it seemed to hover on continually shifting paws. "Pup's a little impatient because we made him wait. Shall we walk while I introduce you? These are my sisters, Arabella and Susan, and my brother Adrian, who claims to be too ill to return to school."

"How do you do?" Gina said politely and found a large, canine nose thrust into her palm. She was used to dogs at home, so let him sniff and then ruffled him under the chin.

"He'll love you forever now," Adrian said with a grin, and then a young lady in black and a familiar gentleman appeared along another path. "And here's Archie. What a surprise."

Catherine ignored him. "I believe you've met Mr. Holles?" she said to Gina, who curtsied to the gentleman's bow. "And this is my closest friend, Miss Hope Darblay."

"She's in mourning," Susan explained unnecessarily.

"And a sort of cousin by marriage," Arabella added.

"Miss Darblay," Gina murmured with interest. The girl looked crushed by all her black crepe, and wistful. "I believe I met your brother last night at Lady Rampton's soiree."

A flash of indignation crossed Miss Darblay's face. "He was there?"

"He was," Catherine said, taking Mr. Holles's arm. "He escorted Mrs. Snodgrass."

"Oh God," Miss Darblay said. "He must be going to do it." She glanced at Gina, flushing slightly. Then her head tilted. "All of London knows our difficulties, so I expect you also know my brother feels compelled to marry a fortune to save the family."

"Actually, I think he may have brought her devilment," Catherine said with unexpected insight. "Just to annoy Lady Rampton. You know how disapproving she always is!"

"Papa has not been dead two months," Miss Darblay said flatly. "Rollo should not be going to parties, as I'm sure all the tabbies were pointing out."

"I think people are making allowances," Mr. Holles said.

"So that he can ruin his life for coin?" Miss Darblay burst out.

"Is he not taking responsibility?" Gina said, then hastily, "Forgive me. This is none of my concern."

A quick smile, alarmingly like Rollo's, caught at Miss Darblay's lips. "I rather think I have made it your concern by bleating about family matters in your company. I should ask for your forgiveness."

"There is no need. Nor should you worry about my discretion. Being trapped with one's own grief and a grieving parent can make one burst out occasionally." She paused, guiltily. "Though I suspect that is not a polite expression."

Miss Darblay laughed. "I like it. And I think it's exactly what

I'm doing. Have you lost a parent, Miss Wallace?"

"My mother. It was several years ago, now, but my father was inconsolable for a long time. The worst of it passes."

"My mother does grieve," Miss Darblay said. "My sister and I grieve. My brother…will not. He is too set on taking the responsibility he never would before. And when he wanted to, my father would never let him."

"Everyone grieves in their own way."

"Yes, but Rollo's will tie him for life to a woman he neither likes nor respects. I cannot believe he will thrive in such a situation."

Gina's stomach twisted. "Have you met Mrs. Snodgrass?"

Hope shuddered. "No, but I saw her in the park once."

"She is a little older than your brother, but I suspect she shares a little of his sense of humor."

Miss Darblay's eyes widened. "You know her?"

"I have spoken to her."

"Is she not appallingly vulgar?"

"Apart from dress choices, no more than I. My father is a Manchester mill owner."

Miss Darblay flushed to the rim of her black bonnet. "I beg your pardon. I meant no disrespect to your family, only to her appearance. It seems I am still bursting out. I shouldn't be saying any of this to a stranger. Your eyes are too kind. And honest."

For a time, they watched the dog chasing sticks thrown by the children and Mr. Holles.

"Would it be easier for you in the country?" Gina suggested.

"My mother will not go. She is too busy pointing Rollo toward heiresses." She sighed. "And I am not the kind to hook a rich man and save him the trouble."

"You're not?" Gina said warily.

"Bookish and dull, with only passable looks and no dowry. No."

In fact, Hope Darblay was rather charmingly pretty, although the black crepe did little to show it.

"He wanted to do it before, you know," Hope said. "Improve the estate. Rollo runs on enthusiasm and that was the one he found when Papa wouldn't buy him a commission. But Papa didn't trust the ideas of a wastrel, even after Oliver—my brother-in-law—let him learn with his steward. I'm afraid if he marries for money, he will go *straight* to the devil thereafter."

Gina looked at her. "Perhaps it is you who doesn't trust him now."

Hope's eyes widened again. "You look at the world differently and aren't afraid to say what you see."

"Have I offended you?"

"Goodness, no."

A piercing whistle rent the air, causing the dog to skid to a halt, head up and ears cocked. A man loped across the grass toward him, hat in hand. It didn't need anyone to say his name for Gina to recognize Rollo Darblay.

Her heartbeat quickened. With the reality, she acknowledged she had hoped to see him here, even before she left the house, and especially after his sister had joined the party. He must have seen her among them, but he only waved his hat at the company in general by way of greeting, while he ruffled the dog's head casually with one hand. Clearly, they were already acquainted.

"What are you doing here?" Hope asked dubiously.

He gave her a crooked smile. "Mama noticed you had gone and sent me after you."

Hope groaned. "Am I not allowed half an hour to myself?"

"Of course you are. I've obeyed and found you. Now I can either shab off again or join the party."

"Join the party!" Susan said with a cheer, and among the laughter, he did. He exchanged a few words with the children, threw a stick for the dog, and bantered with Catherine and Mr. Holles with the ease of old friendship.

Then he walked beside Gina and Hope, occasionally veering to play with the dog. It reminded Gina of their carefree day in the pleasure gardens at Maida, before she had complicated everything. His company was just as beguiling now—friendly, amusing, irreverent, and often surprising. She could never afterward remember what they had talked about, what he had said, but by the time they all parted ways, she felt relaxed and content once more.

And just a little excited, for he had asked everyone if they would be at the Carringtons' ball this evening. Of course, he was in mourning. He shouldn't be attending balls, but somehow, she didn't put it past him.

※※※

As Little helped Gina dress for her first grand ball, the maid's face was a mask of lofty disapproval. At last, Gina sighed. "Very well, out with it, Little. What have I done to incur your wrath?"

"If you don't know, Miss—"

"If I knew, I wouldn't be asking."

Little jabbed in a hairpin with unnecessary force. "That swaggering fellow. The one in the park. He was at Renwick's Hotel."

Damn. There was still nothing wrong with Little's powers of observation. How much had she seen? "Yes, I went for a walk with him." *And danced with him. And went to his bed...*

"Lord Longton wouldn't like it."

"If his lordship did not wish me to associate with London society, he would not have suggested I come," Gina said, rising to her feet. "And frankly, Little, this is hard enough without you spying and scolding."

"Spying!" Little gasped, affronted.

"The sapphire set, if you please."

Little, who had always been given the privileges of an old retainer and made full use of them, all but gawped at her. But Gina had had enough. If she was adult enough to be sold for a title, then she would at least be treated with the respect due to a lady, not a naughty child.

Downstairs, Mrs. Fitzwilliam fussed and preened over her, and Fitz showed a gratifying tendency to goggle. From which she gathered she looked good enough to impress. She tried not to examine who this impression was aimed at, beyond her fellow guests. Lord Longton would be there, of course, as would Miss Dove and Mr. Holles. Fitz asked gallantly for the first dance, for which she was grateful since she had no desire to be a wallflower. Lord Longton had already told her he did not dance. For which she was also secretly grateful.

As it turned out, Lord Longton was the first person she noticed on entering the glittering ballroom. Although Gina had never seen so many bejeweled people in one place before, his lordship stood out, close to the door, in conversation with Lord Sedgemoor and a couple of other older gentlemen.

He saw her immediately and bowed. She inclined her head and then several people swept into the space between them. It came to Gina that he was still assessing her worthiness to be Lady Longton. He might want her money and her youth to bear him sons, but he would consider only a ladylike wife. She knew a defiant urge to shriek with laughter and stomp rather than glide across the floor as she had been taught.

And then she saw Rollo, prowling the floor as though looking for someone. *Me?*

"What is young Darblay doing here?" Mrs. Fitzwilliam exclaimed. "He really is not taking his mourning seriously, is he?"

"He did for a month," Fitz defended. "Mostly. I daresay he won't dance."

"No, he'll be in the card room losing the shirt off his back. Oh, look, Gina, there is Princess Hagerin. She is the widow of some German princeling, I believe, although everyone was surprised she married him and not Dearham. In any case, she is frightfully fashionable and just a little fast, but I should probably introduce you... Princess, how do you do? Allow me to present my protegee, Miss Wallace."

Princess Hagerin was one of these devastatingly attractive

women whom no one notices is not actually beautiful. She smiled graciously at Gina. "I believe I saw you at Lady Rampton's the other night. Admiring Mr. Dornan's portraits with Lord Longton."

Gina's own smile became fixed, for the princess's eyes were extremely shrewd. "I liked the portraits very much, though I'm afraid I did not recognize many of them."

"Oh, you will. Lord Longton should ask Mr. Dornan for a likeness of him. You will come to my Venetian breakfast, will you not, Mrs. Fitzwilliam?"

"Of course. We are looking forward to it."

As the princess drifted onward, Gina was left with the feeling that she was meant to have understood something from the encounter, though she wasn't sure what it was.

In any case, there followed another bewildering array of introductions, curtsies, and smiles, so it was a relief when the dancing opened, and she could join Fitz in a country dance. She enjoyed dancing, so her vague feeling of oppression lifted. Until she saw Rollo once more, almost plastered to the side of an astonishingly beautiful young woman in pink.

ROLLO HAD JUST seen Gina joining the dance set with Fitz when he was ambushed by Miss Smythe and her mother. Their appearance took him entirely by surprise, for he hadn't considered Mrs. Carrington would invite them. Fortunately, he was not obliged to dance with her, being in mourning, though at least the dance would have kept her to a proper distance more of the time. He'd had very naughty ladybirds who behaved with more decorum in public, he thought austerely, though it was not something he could say to the girl clutching his arm to her bosom.

Instead, he said, "Here, this is more the thing." And prizing her hand off his upper arm, he set it on the sleeve of his lower arm instead, using his elbow to fend her off to a safer distance.

She pouted. "Anyone would think you didn't want to be close to me."

Anyone would be right. "You'll get the kind of reputation you don't want," he said bluntly.

"Like yours?" she asked, fluttering her eyelashes.

"Yes. Which does a lady more harm than it ever will me."

"Not if she was Lady Darblay, surely?"

"You're not. And my mother is always a lady." Apart from the gambling and an excessive fondness for sherry, but this was not something Miss Smythe needed to know.

Her eyes spat venom for a moment, then she smiled. "I was only jesting, silly. It's awfully crowded in here, is it not?" She wafted her fan. "I might need air."

"Then I shall return you to your mother, who is better able to deal with fainting fits."

She subsided once more, and before the dance had properly ended, he was able to fob her off on Calton, who was an earl and therefore outranked him. And Calton was more than able to take care of himself.

Free of her, he felt like dusting off his hands. All the same, he didn't like her possessiveness. She really had thought he was in her pocket, and the needing air comment was clearly an effort to get him alone where, presumably, they would be discovered in a compromising position.

He should have been flattered, for no woman had ever pursued him to that extent before. Instead, he shuddered and watched Gina Wallace cross the floor on Fitz's arm. Longton awaited her beside Mrs. Fitzwilliam and handed her into a chair beside his.

"Stop scowling, Rollo, you look like Lord Byron," said a voice at his side. "Who is she?"

Rollo turned in some surprise to face his brother-in-law. "Wenning?" He thrust out his hand, and Lord Wenning shook it.

"What are you doing here? Is Grace in town, too?"

"Yes, I left her with Hope and your mama. She seemed to think Hope needed a little…company. She's trying to persuade them both to come back with us."

"That would be an excellent idea."

"Come, too, if you like." The offer was made casually, by a man Rollo had once despised for making his sister miserable, but whom he now liked and grudgingly respected. Oliver Harlaw, Earl of Wenning, was also living proof that one could mature into sense and understanding without becoming a bore.

"I'd like to," Rollo said with a touch of wistfulness, "but I have to see to my own estates."

"Your mother believes she has to oversee your marriage. Hope believes she has to make sure you *don't* marry."

"It's nothing to do with either of them," Rollo said.

"Or me?" Wenning suggested, easily reading the unspoken message. "My interest is purely impersonal. Who is she?"

"I don't know what you mean."

"Who inspired the Byronic scowl?"

"Lord, no one in particular. Just the whole situation. For example, see the beauty dancing with Calton? She is one of my mother's favored choices."

Wenning followed his gaze. "A diamond of the first water," he agreed.

"She's delightful from a distance. Anyway, what *are* you doing here without Grace? Did my mother send you to be sure I went about my mercenary courtships aright?"

"I imagine she thinks she did."

Rollo gave a reluctant grin. "You're a devious creature, Wenning. God knows why my sister puts up with you."

"Game of piquet?" Wenning suggested.

"Why not?" Rollo said and walked with him across to the card room.

While Rollo dealt the cards, Wenning placed two glasses on the table and sat opposite him. They didn't discuss what they were playing for. They both understood Rollo *couldn't* pay, and Wenning would neither ask nor cheat in his brother-in-law's favor.

"Why are *you* here?" Wenning asked as they began to play. "If the heiress isn't the draw, who is?"

Rollo's lips twisted. "Another heiress, if you must know. And one I can't marry."

"Why not?"

"Because she's betrothed to another. Play."

"Rollo," Wenning said with oddly kind mockery. "Faint heart never won fair lady." Before Rollo could retort, Wenning, glancing toward the door, fixed his gaze. "And that has to be the famous Mrs. Snodgrass."

"Lord, is she here, too? Mrs. Carrington has thrown her net wide."

"Hope says you escorted her to Lady Rampton's soiree last night."

Rollo grinned. "It was worth it. In any case, she's worth several Lady Ramptons. And I'm not talking about money."

Wenning looked interested but continued to play. After a few moments, he murmured, "You don't need to do it, you know. I can loan you enough to pay your debts and make a start on the land."

Once, Rollo would have grabbed it with both hands and laughed. Now, he smiled a little ruefully at the cards. "My family has taken more than enough from you."

"But I have Grace," Wenning replied. "The rest is nothing. And seriously, Rollo, it would be no hardship."

"Thanks," Rollo muttered. He met Wenning's gaze. "Seems I'm trapped between one dishonor or another. But I will think about your offer." Which was more than he had done the first time it was made.

Since Meade and Fitz wandered over shortly afterward, confidences were postponed.

Chapter Nine

Strolling around the ballroom on Lord Longton's arm, Gina was discovering that her betrothed possessed his share of contradictions. She was loathe to call them hypocrisies.

When she remarked, most casually, on the beauty of the girl waltzing with Lord Calton—the same girl who had previously been clutching Rollo's arm during the previous dance—he pronounced. "She's pretty enough, I grant you, but she smells of the shop. Her mother's trying to palm her off on a title when neither of them have any business at a ton party."

From which Gina gathered the girl's family were in trade and looked for a noble husband for her. Much the same case as Gina, in fact, though Longton seemed oblivious.

When a lady came out of the card room, crossing their path, and Gina asked politely if he cared for cards, he replied, "Indeed, I am very fond of cards and dice, though they are hardly a proper diversion for ladies."

Gina did not bother to ask why. She was trying not to stare at Rollo Darblay, who sat at a piquet table with a distinguished gentleman.

Lord Longton, it seemed, had high standards where other people were concerned, so she couldn't help wondering what he would think when they came upon Mrs. Snodgrass again. With a hint of defiance, Gina paused to speak to her and introduced Lord

Longton in case he chose not to remember their meeting at Lady Rampton's.

To Gina's surprise, his lordship was perfectly gracious. From the ensuing conversation, Gina gathered that Mrs. Snodgrass had two sons away at school. Longton, the father of two daughters, commiserated on the difficulty of being a sole parent.

Mrs. Snodgrass nodded. "You talk like a sensible man," she allowed in apparent surprise.

Gina, afraid to look at his lordship in case his haughtiness set her off into fits of giggles, was highly relieved to be interrupted by Mr. Montague, asking if he might have the pleasure of the ensuing dance.

Gina was happy to accept, not least because she knew him to be a friend of Rollo's. But he proved to be an extremely good-natured young man, happy to chatter on any subject whenever the dance brought them together. Afterward, he conducted her back to Mrs. Fitzwilliam, who introduced her to another young man who immediately asked her to dance.

At least I am not a wallflower, she thought with some surprise. Presumably, word of her fortune had got out and outweighed her lowly birth in more eyes than Lord Longton's. She would have enjoyed herself more had she not been sure that Rollo was avoiding her. So, when the dance ended and her partner offered to escort her back to Mrs. Fitzwilliam, she was glad to run into Catherine Dove, who immediately slipped her arm through hers.

"Thank you," Gina said to her partner. "But I believe I will just walk with Miss Dove for a few moments first. Is there fresh air?" she added to Catherine as her escort walked away disconsolate.

"Of course. There's a little terrace out here."

"You don't miss much, do you?" Gina said with amusement as Catherine guided her straight to an open French door.

"Well, when one is young and engaged, it can be difficult to be alone with one's betrothed."

I wouldn't know. I am older than you and have no desire to be alone with my betrothed. The thought was exquisitely sad, so she turned her mind instead to the pleasure of the fresh air and the gentle breeze instead.

"When will you be married?" she asked idly.

"Not until the autumn. Our parents decided on a longer engagement because we are both young and our attachment was quite sudden."

Gina smiled. "You are content."

"And happy. Archie is wonderful."

"I shall tell him you said so," came a male voice, and a tall, distinguished man emerged from the shadows onto the lit part of the terrace. He might have been the man she had seen playing cards with Rollo.

"My lord!" Catherine exclaimed, allowing the stranger to bend and kiss her cheek. "I did not know you were here! Is Cousin Grace with you?"

"She is at home with her mother and Hope. I'm really just keeping out of their way. I'd ask how you are, but you are clearly blooming. Won't you present me to your friend?"

"Gina, this is my cousin, Lord Wenning," Catherine said obediently. "Cousin, my friend Miss Wallace."

Lord Wenning bowed over Gina's proffered hand. This was Rollo's brother-in-law, she realized, and she had heard his name before. He was a diplomat, whose successful missions had been lauded in the newspapers. And yet she doubted he was as much as thirty years old.

"Enchanted," he murmured, bowing over her hand.

"Playing chaperone, my lord?" inquired yet another newcomer. Mr. Holles joined them on the otherwise empty terrace, a sardonic curl to his lips.

"Seeking a moment's respite from the festivities within," Wenning responded. "As it appears, are you."

"Of course," Mr. Holles said stiffly, although it was quite clear to everyone by then that he and Catherine Dove had an assignation.

Lord Wenning's lips twitched. "Don't mind me. I shall merely sit here and make conversation with Miss Wallace, secure in the certainty that I will hear or see nothing to upset my—er…nerves."

Catherine stuck her nose in the air, not entirely in jest, Gina thought, and took her betrothed's arm to perambulate the length of the terrace.

"Dear me," Lord Wenning said, assisting Gina onto the bench, "I appear to be presiding over an assignation. I hope I am not interrupting another."

Gina met his gaze. "No. Not if you mean me."

"Forgive me. Since we are only just acquainted, I have no idea whether or not you are also betrothed or even married."

"No," Gina replied, although honesty compelled her to admit, "Not formally, but there is an understanding."

"Ah. One of those. May I know the lucky gentleman?"

"It is not my place to say."

His eyebrows flew up. "Really?"

She withstood his gaze, but he only smiled and drew her attention to the beauty of the sky, and from there, light, unthreatening conversation flowed. He was both witty and engaging, so she had no idea when Catherine and Mr. Holles returned to the ballroom.

A waltz was playing, which probably explained it.

"Thank you for your company," Gina said rising quickly. "I should return to Mrs. Fitzwilliam who will be wondering where I have got to."

Wenning rose at once, making no effort to detain her. "May I escort you to her?" His gaze drifted over her head. "On the other hand, perhaps there is no need."

Gina whirled around to see Rollo striding toward them, glowering. "Wenning, what the devil do you mean by—"

"Nothing, dear boy. Nothing at all." Wenning smiled amiably and bowed to Gina. "Unless you object, I'll leave Darblay to escort you inside."

As he sauntered away to the ballroom, Rollo scowled after him. "What the deuce did he want?"

"I think he came to keep an eye on Miss Dove and Mr. Holles. And took pity on me as the gooseberry."

"If he overstepped—"

"He didn't," Gina interrupted, although it did strike her that Lord Wenning might have had other reasons of his own for spending time with her.

With an apparent effort, Rollo banished his frown. "Will you dance with me?"

"You're in mourning. You must have told innumerable people you aren't dancing this evening. They will talk if you now dance with me."

Rollo sighed. "True enough and…" He broke off and smiled, seizing her by the hand. "Not if they don't see you." He drew her only half-protesting to the far side of the terrace and down the side of the house. A splash of moonlight illuminated a long, narrow kitchen garden, and another small terrace.

Rollo spun her into his arms and began to waltz. She laughed, because it reminded her of their illicit dances at Maida Gardens and because the music, while fainter here than at the front, was still compelling.

And Rollo's arms were bliss. No one else felt so wonderful or smelled so enticing. And he held her too close. The movement of his hips and thighs against her body spread a sweet, heavy heat that was all too familiar. All of her remembered all of him. She wanted to lay her head on his broad chest.

"I know it isn't what we agreed," he murmured into her hair. "But I think about you all the time. I can't help it."

She closed her eyes. "Don't, Rollo," she said shakily. "You will marry Mrs. Snodgrass, or someone else, and save your family and your people. I will marry Lord Longton and make my father proud."

"I know. I know. But do you ever think of me?"

All the time. She raised her head, meaning to flee ignominiously from this temptation, but his face swooped down, and his mouth took hers. A sob broke from her, because she wanted this so much, and it was wrong. But even at the height of their passion in the hotel, he had never kissed her like this, with such blatant hunger.

She had to clutch him before her knees gave way. His kiss, the movements of his body, no longer dancing but desiring, arousing, battered her senses. She could only welcome him, opening wide to his onslaught and kissing him back with equal ferocity. He slid a knee between her legs, and she let out a soft moan of pleasure and need, pressing against him.

Just as she thought he would devour her utterly, he gentled the kiss, seducing her instead with heart-breaking tenderness. "Forgive me," he whispered against her lips. "I think I am half-mad, but I would never hurt you."

"I'm not hurt." To prove it, she kissed his lips once more. "But Rollo, we cannot do this, nothing like this ever again."

The tragedy nearly broke her heart and had him crushing her mouth desperately beneath his once more. So, she kissed him back, one very last time. And that was when a silent figure rushed out of nowhere and slammed into her, sending her flying against the stone wall of the house.

Stunned and disoriented, she saw the beautiful girl in pink that she had noticed in the ballroom. In the moonlight, the girl hurled herself against Rollo, locking both arms around his neck. If Gina had not been so bewildered, the pain twisting through her would no doubt have been sharper.

And then, blessedly irritable, came Rollo's voice. "Get *off* me!"

"She won't have you, she won't! She's from the *north*! And you are *my* viscount!" The girl was in a total, childish tantrum.

"Pull yourself together," Gina said sharply. "I have seen babies with more manners. His lordship is not a toy to squabble over."

Whether Gina's words would have made any difference, she

never discovered. Certainly, the girl paused long enough to stare at her over Rollo's shoulder, but by then two men had arrived, grasping an arm each and hauled her off Rollo.

"Wenning's holding up her mother," Mr. Montague said. "It's a trap to pretend you compromised her. Get the lady inside, and Meade and I will chaperone each other."

Rollo was dusting off his shoulders as he approached Gina. "Are you hurt?" he asked, low.

"No, just startled…"

"Come, then." He placed her hand in his arm and waited only long enough to say to the furious beauty. "If I were you, I would faint. And neither of them has a title."

"Goodness," Gina said y as they walked smartly to the corner of the main terrace. "Does this kind of thing happen to you often?"

"Never," Rollo said grimly. "Until word spread that I'm hanging out for a rich wife. One of your pins on the right is loosened."

Gina found it with her fingers, captured the errant lock of hair, and shoved the pin back in. A few people had now gathered on the terrace, no doubt as the ballroom grew warmer. From among them, came Lord Wenning, towed along by a middle-aged, blue-gowned lady in a tearing hurry.

"Ah, Darblay," Lord Wenning drawled. "Ma'am." He bowed to Gina. "This lady has lost her daughter. Perhaps you have seen her."

"Miss Smythe?" Rollo lied blatantly. "No, not since earlier in the evening."

"Hmm, is this the young lady, perhaps?" Wenning inquired.

Gina risked a glance and glimpsed Miss Smythe, the back of her hand to her forehead, being solicitously conducted toward her mother by Mr. Meade and Mr. Montague.

"I suppose it's funny," Rollo said without a great deal of humor as they walked back inside the ballroom.

"No," Gina said slowly. "No, it isn't. It's intolerable."

His frown was back as he glanced down at her, along with

concern that warmed her heart. But they were in a ballroom full of people, the vast majority of whom had nothing better to do than gossip. She thought he swore under his breath, then he muttered, "I have to take you back to your aunt or there will be talk. You still have choices, Gina."

She rubbed her forehead above the eyes. "I need to think."

"We can't talk here," he muttered. "Tomorrow afternoon. I'll get Hope and Catherine to take you walking in the park again."

And then she was back with Mrs. Fitzwilliam, who didn't look best pleased to see her in Rollo's company, though she was perfectly polite. Rollo didn't stay but strode back toward the card room.

THE CARD ROOM emptied considerably as the supper dance formed. Rollo, who had found his friends in possession of a brandy bottle, was relieved. The extra space meant he could sprawl with his glass among his gaming friends. In a few minutes. Meade and Montague came in, winked reassuringly at Rollo, and joined Fitz and Lord Dominic Gorse at the table.

Rollo flexed his shoulders, trying to concentrate on the cards rather than on Gina.

It wasn't easy, since he was only watching, not playing, and since her scent was still in his nostrils, her taste on his lips, the feel of her soft, yielding body pressed passionately to his…

But even the physical arousal was a distraction from what mattered.

"*It is intolerable.*" She was about to give herself in marriage, put herself completely into the power of a man she did not, could not like. Watching her with him, he had known that, known it was wrong, wishing he could do something. But now she had actually said the words, acknowledging this whole situation was intolerable for both of them.

"*Faint heart never won fair lady.*"

Wenning is right. I need to do something, Even if she never speaks to me again, I can't let her throw her whole life away with this ridiculous marriage.

"My Lord Darblay!"

It still felt odd to be addressed so. Lord Darblay was his father. But the urgency of the voice made him look him up at the speaker anyway. A clearly furious young man, holding himself rigid, glared at Rollo.

"That's me," Rollo acknowledged with a silent salute to his late parent.

"You may not recall, my lord, but we met at Mrs. Smythe's on Wednesday afternoon."

"Ah, thought you looked familiar," Rollo said cheerfully, and not quite truthfully. "Pull up a chair."

"What I have to say, my lord, would be better said in private," the young man said stiffly.

"Better lower your voice, then," Rollo advised, glancing around at the scattering of people in the room, several of whom were glancing in their direction. He hooked a chair leg with his foot and dragged it to the table. "Sit and tell me what I can do for you."

The young man sat, looking slightly bewildered, though his shoulders quickly straightened again and his scowl reformed. "You can meet me, sir!"

He spoke in low but furious tones, and Rollo's friends all stopped playing to look and listen.

"Meet you where?" Rollo asked for devilment. "White's? Your gaff or mine? Depends what you want to do, I suppose."

The young man spoke through his teeth. "I want, sir, to punish you for your ill-treatment of a lady!"

Miss Smythe. Even for her, this was quick work. "Don't be silly," Rollo said. "Have a drink and tell me quietly—very quietly and without naming names for God's sake—what you think I've done."

"You have dishonored a young and very beautiful lady," the

man hissed as Dominic Gorse pushed a glass into his hand.

"Pretty sure I didn't," Rollo said.

"Depends on your definition of *dishonored*," Meade said unhelpfully. "And lady, come to that. Was this a long time ago?"

The young man frowned at him. "No, it was not! Less than an hour ago."

"No," Meade said with certainty. "Got the wrong man."

"I was not," the young man said dangerously, "talking to you but to his lordship."

"Look," Rollo interrupted. "You've got the wrong end of the stick. Come and see me tomorrow because we can't talk about it here."

"I don't want to talk about it," the young man declared, setting his untouched glass firmly on the table. "I am calling you out, sir."

"Don't be daft. I'm not fighting with you."

"Should have come a few years ago," Meade said nostalgically. "Always in a fight, then."

"You're foxed, Meade," Lord Dominic uttered. "It's as well the bottle's empty."

The angry young man was not distracted. If anything, he was even more furious. In fact, he made a grab for the glass he had recently put down, no doubt to dash it in Rollo's face.

Rollo was quicker. He closed his hand around the boy's wrist, making sure he could not lift it. The liquid slopped up the sides of the glass but did not spill.

"Don't be an idiot," Rollo said below his breath. "If you throw that over me, the whole world will know it and speculate. It won't be long until the name you imagine you're protecting will be all over London. How much good will that do her?"

"Then you will meet me!"

"I will not."

The boy stared at him. "Because you imagine I am beneath you? Or that she is?"

"Neither, you imbecile. Because there is nothing to fight

about."

In desperation, the boy turned to Rollo's friends. "What is the matter with him? Is he a coward? Too full of his own nobility to fight a banker's son?"

"Don't push your luck," Lord Dominic advised softly.

The young man glared at him defiantly. "Very well. I am told his lordship is no stranger to duels, so I can only suppose it is my lack of noble blood that troubles him."

"No," Rollo said, uneasily aware that the room was almost silent. A couple of gentlemen had stood up and were trying to hover a bit nearer to hear.

"Well, my lord? Can I expect to hear from you?"

"Yes, yes," Rollo said testily. "For God's sake go away."

The young man stood and dropped a card on the table before walking off, his back rigid.

Rollo swore softly but fluently.

"Not sure you'll be able to keep this quiet," Lord Dominic murmured. "Whatever it's about."

Rollo lifted his brandy glass. "It's been a busy evening," he observed.

CHAPTER TEN

MEADE AND MONTAGUE were already in Rollo's dressing room at midday, drinking coffee when Fitz and Lord Dominic were shown in.

"Well?" Rollo demanded.

"He won't budge," Fitz said cheerfully.

"He did accept us as seconds," Dominic said, "once we explained the sense of keeping the lady's name between the six of us. But he wouldn't believe that you were innocent of her charges and won't withdraw his challenge."

"Idiot," Rollo fumed. "I have enough to do without this. Can't he see what the girl's like?"

"Vindictive little liar?" Dominic said sardonically. "I suppose she couldn't be persuaded to tell this lad—what's his name?"

"James Black. His father owns Black's Bank."

"Would she tell Black the truth once she understands she could be signing his death warrant?"

"Or Rollo's," Montague pointed out.

"I suppose she might have calmed down by now," Rollo said dubiously. "And she can't marry me if I'm dead."

"You won't be dead," Meade said. "You've never lost a duel. But if you kill him, you'll have to leave the country."

"There is that," Rollo said with a certain amount of longing. He could flee with Gina, live in France or Italy… He sighed. "I don't want to kill the gudgeon. But I doubt Miss Smythe cares if he lives or not, so long as she can get at me. I suppose… As the challenged party, I get to choose weapons, so I could make it swords and first blood wins."

"Won't stop a whole party setting up at Putney Heath to see the fun," Dominic foretold. "Your Mr. Black was not entirely discreet."

"I expect Miss Smythe's name is already linked to the quarrel, too," Fitz said. "More than one person must have seen her overcome on the terrace. And you were in the vicinity."

"With another woman entirely," Montague pointed out. "Though I suppose that would become lost."

Rollo scowled. "Keep it that way. I'll not have *her* name dragged into this. And if everyone wants to waste their time at Putney, arrange it somewhere else."

"Where?" Dominic asked.

Rollo stood and reached for his coat. "I don't know, but I'll think about it. Finish the coffee if you want. I have an appointment. Escorting Hope to meet some friends."

"Miss Wallace!" Mrs. Snodgrass sounded genuinely surprised as she welcomed Gina into a room that appeared to be half-drawing room, half-study.

Gina took the proffered hand. "Thank you for seeing me. I know it's early for a morning call."

"Not for me. I don't lie abed half the day. I have work to do. Please, sit down, and I'll ring for tea."

"Not for me, ma'am. I have an appointment, so I won't trouble you for long." Gina caught herself twisting her skirts between her fingers and forced them to stop. She looked directly at her amiable but curious hostess who had sat on the other side of the sofa. "You will think me impertinent, Mrs. Snodgrass."

"If I do, I'll tell you. Are you related to Robert Wallace, of Wallace and Son in Manchester?"

"He is my father."

"Then I expect your reasons for the Season's festivities are much the same as mine. There's only one thing left to do when you've made as much money as Robert Wallace and me. And that's to seek acceptance for your children among the highest of the land. That involves marriage, rather like a commercial transaction. I don't let 'em pretend otherwise. But I think the whole business bothers you. You're younger, of course."

"And it was not my idea," Gina admitted.

"And now you're supposed to marry Longton, and you don't like it."

Gina, who was still feeling her way toward a half-formed plan, let that remark go. "My impertinent question is this. Do you love Lord Darblay?"

Mrs. Snodgrass smiled. "Darblay? He's handsome, young, impudent, and fun. What is there not to like?"

Oh, he is more, so much more than that… "That wasn't my question, ma'am," Gina pointed out.

Mrs. Snodgrass was silent, searching Gina's face. "I'm ten years his senior, at least. I have two sons almost grown. Darblay is a rogue, but however wicked, he is a boy to me. My Snoddy was not a boy."

"You still love your late husband," Gina said gently.

"I do. But I will still take another. As for you… It is not fair if you don't have a choice. Just make sure you don't pick another wrong one in retaliation. Think carefully on whatever you are about."

"I will," Gina assured her, rising to her feet. "And you have helped me a great deal."

"I have?" Mrs. Snodgrass looked baffled. "Well, let me know if I can help further."

Gina smiled. "I might just call upon you. Thank you, ma'am. Goodbye!"

Deep in thought, she hurried through Mayfair toward Hyde Park. The germ of an idea that had been gnawing at her since returning to the ballroom last night, after Miss Smythe's little fracas, was growing apace and bringing with it the same sense of reckless excitement and purpose. Much like the notion of inviting the viscount to bed her.

She had not properly understood the ramifications of that invitation. She had been aware that, in different circumstances, she could have fallen in love with Rollo Darblay. That had been the root of her proposal. To give her just one memory of love to cherish in the difficult years ahead.

But it wasn't enough. She had bargained without the bonds that their delicious intimacy seemed to have woven around them, and without *feelings*, which refused to do as they were told. In retrospect, her idea had been naïve and dangerous. For it seemed wrong in every conceivable way to marry one man while loving another. To let Rollo tie himself for life to someone else.

It was nearly time for her father to announce her betrothal. So time was running out. That reckless little seed was sending out shoots all over the place and growing apace.

"Miss Wallace?"

Gina paused, blinking to drag herself back to the present. She had walked through the gates of Hyde Park and a large, excited dog was dancing about in front of her, shoving its nose into her hand. She petted it absently, while she took in the group of people she hadn't known she was meeting—Catherine Dove and her siblings, Hope Darblay…and the viscount whom she *had* come to meet. Preserving her reputation, he had brought her trustworthy chaperones.

His consideration warmed the smile already spreading involuntarily across her face at the sight of him. And just for an instant, he reminded her of the moment he had first looked up at her in the ladies' lounge, astonished, confused, almost *dazzled*. Although there was something much warmer in his eyes now that she felt right down to her toes, a smile playing on those sinful, passionate lips.

Hastily, she forced out words of greeting and curtseyed to the company, which then set off in jolly fashion. Catherine led the way toward a quiet area of the park where there was enough open grass for the dog to run. There was also a bench where two people could sit comfortably, part of a group and yet distant enough to be private when everyone else played with the dog. Gina suspected Catherine came here frequently with Mr. Holles.

Today, however, Lord Darblay handed Gina onto the seat and sat beside her, one arm over the back of the bench as he turned toward her.

"Don't do it," he said abruptly.

She didn't pretend to misunderstand him. "Marry Longton?"

"It's the only life you have. Don't waste it on him."

She waited, her heart beating fast, but he didn't repeat the offer he had made at the hotel. *"If your father wants a noble fortune hunter, have me instead."* No offer, no declaration of love.

She swallowed, trying not to let the hurt swamp her need to know, and gazed up at the sky. "What do you think would have happened, Rollo, if we had met in different circumstances? If I were not wealthy and engaged, and you were not hanging out for a rich wife?"

"Exactly what *has* happened between us." He frowned. "Except you wouldn't have invited me to bed you. And I *probably* wouldn't have done it. I could have courted you."

She risked a glance at him. "If we had been able to marry, would you have kept your ladybirds?"

A groan of laughter broke from him. "Gina, I wouldn't even have *thought* of them. Don't you know that?"

Warmth seeped into her anxious heart at the endearment as much as the sentiment. Her heart ached because he looked at once so wonderfully rakish and handsome and honest, and he was not hers. Not yet. "Life isn't fair, is it?"

"No. You just have to make the best of it."

"For everyone," she said frowning. She risked a glance at him.

"My father gave his word to Longton."

Rollo's lips tightened. His eyes spat. "He had no right."

This was even more encouraging. Her heart lifted further. "Legally, he had not. I am of age. But I did go along with it, and I would hate to be responsible for his breaking his word for the first time ever."

Rollo threw himself against the back of the bench. "So you told me," he said savagely.

"I wanted to know," she said, forcing herself to keep watching him when the cowardly part of her was afraid to see, "if you thought it would be a good idea for *Longton* to break his word."

His gaze flew to hers. He sat up again, his eyes devouring her. "I think it would be the best idea you've ever had, including the one at Maida. But how would we make him do that?"

Her heart almost burst. *We.* He had said *"we."* "I haven't quite worked that out yet, but he has quite definite ideas of what he doesn't want in a wife. I just have to convince him I have those foibles in spades."

Fierce laughter gleamed in Rollo's eyes. "You are quite unexpectedly *bad* on occasion. This is why—"

"Rollo, look out!" Hope called just as a stick flew over their heads, and the massive dog, approaching at high speed, threatened to leap after it. Gina and Rollo scattered to either side, laughing.

Part of her was infuriated, because Rollo might just have been about to say, *"This is why I love you."* But in truth, she didn't need the words. She already knew.

"THERE YOU ARE," exclaimed Mrs. Fitzwilliam when she returned to the house. "Come into the drawing room. You just missed Lord Longton, and all the servants knew was that you had gone to walk in the park with friends. You did not even take Little!"

"Oh, I left early, and she was up so late last night to undress me," Gina said truthfully. Not that she had wanted Little to know she had visited Mrs. Snodgrass or held a long, private conversation with Lord Darblay. A wonderful conversation with Lord Darblay. She sat down opposite Mrs. Fitzwilliam and asked brightly. "Did Lord Longton disapprove of my unaccompanied expedition?"

"Don't be silly. I wasn't foolish enough to tell him it was unaccompanied. I told him it was with the Doves, so I hope that was correct."

"It was," Gina said.

"Good. Well, you will be pleased to know that he is delighted with the way you are progressing in society. He called you a most graceful and unaffected girl with excellent manners and no foolish airs."

"How kind of him." Gina tried to keep the panic from her voice. It struck her that Longton might well have come to formalize their betrothal. She could only pray he would do nothing before speaking with her. But it made her plans much more urgent. She sat forward. "Tell me about his lordship, ma'am. You must have known him for years."

"Well, yes, we have always moved in the same circles. In fact, as you know, it was I who introduced him to your dear father."

And like everyone else, she had imagined she was doing Gina and her family a good turn. "He seems a man of some contradictions," Gina said carefully. "Very high in the instep, although he is considering a mill-owner's daughter as his wife."

"You have no vulgarity about you. You are a ladylike lady."

Not in Rollo Darblay's bed. "He loves gaming," Gina pursued, "and yet disapproves of it for ladies. Even you gamble, Mrs. Fitz."

"There is nothing wrong with ladies playing cards and gambling in moderation," Mrs. Fitzwilliam pronounced. "But his lordship's little foible is understandable. His first wife was addicted to the gaming tables and lost a small fortune."

"Then it was his *wife* who gambled away their fortune?"

"She certainly didn't help. But no, I don't think we can blame it entirely on her. That doesn't mean," Mrs. Fitzwilliam added hastily, "that he has not learned the error of his ways. He is an older and wiser man now."

"Of course. What else does he dislike in a lady?"

"Any breath of scandal," Mrs. Fitzwilliam replied at once. "Which is one reason I thought of you. You were always such a well-behaved and dutiful girl. And he dislikes untidiness of any sort—about one's person or one's abode. He once gave an amiable gentleman the cut direct for having a mere drop of sauce on his cravat! And he rejected at least one prospective wife for sitting on a sofa surrounded by two novels, her needlework, and a writing desk. He dislikes the smell of horse and cannot abide pet animals."

Gina's breath caught. "How…helpful. Tell me more, Mrs. Fitz."

⸻

ROLLO, SINCE HE still held membership, strolled round to White's to meet his friends for dinner and learn the latest about the irritation that was his latest duel.

He found Meade and Montague drinking brandy with Fitz. Dominic Gorse was not present, being a married man who liked to spend time with his wife. Wenning was the same. Something else Rollo better understood, now.

"He won't budge," Fitz greeted him. "Won't admit he was in the wrong."

"And obviously we can't apologize for something you didn't do," Meade put in.

"So, stalemate there," Fitz said. "But he *has* agreed to the unusual venue of our choice."

"What unusual venue?" Rollo asked without much interest. He was thinking about Gina and ways to make Longton cry off the engagement.

"Maida Gardens."

That got his attention. "Maida?" A breath of laughter shook him, though he didn't quite know why, unless because it was where he had met Gina and it seemed like good luck. "Can we get into the gardens at that time of the morning?"

"Not easily, but there's a decent meadow at the side, and Renwick's Hotel is handy for breakfast afterward."

"Very true," Rollo agreed, much struck by this sensible arrangement. "And he was fine about swords?"

"Well, he went a bit white when Dom told him that was your choice," Fitz replied. "So, I suspect he lacks experience in fencing."

Rollo sighed. "Well, I'll get it over with quickly, and we can move on. The Smythe girl isn't spreading this story about town, is she?"

"She might have, more fool her." Montague shook his head. "She doesn't seem to realize a duel over her will ruin her in polite society. But no one should know about Maida. Best we can do."

By evening, Gina had several possible plans in her head, though they all resulted in the ruin of her reputation, which she could not countenance for her family's sake if not her own. She retired early, in the hope that sleep would bring wisdom.

Unfortunately, it didn't. But as she waited in the hall for Mrs. Fitzwilliam—they were due to attend Princess Hagerin's Venetian breakfast—the butler picked up the morning post and handed her a letter in her father's hand.

She sat down on the nearest chair and broke the seal. As she scanned the letter, a stifled groan escaped her lips, and then, as she read on, she began to smile.

"Good news?" Mrs. Fitzwilliam asked, bustling toward her.

"From Papa," Gina said, handing her the letter. "He is on his way to London and proposes to stop for a night, as we did, at Renwick's Hotel. I told him in my last letter about the delightful music at the pleasure garden, and he proposes we join him there for a few hours."

"He proposes first that we meet him there and dine at the hotel the night before," Mrs. Fitzwilliam pointed out, saving Gina the trouble. "Which is quite an unnecessary expense."

"Oh, Papa would cover it easily. He has not been in London for years, and it is a treat for him. It will be tomorrow night, though. Do we have any commitments?"

"Only the theatre, which hardly matters. But, my dear, the pleasure garden is hardly fashionable…"

"But it will be fun," Gina coaxed. "And do you know, I think Fitz might enjoy it, too, so we could ask him to escort us."

"It doesn't really seem like Godfrey's cup of tea," his aunt said. "But, yes, we can ask him. I'll write him a note when we come back."

The princess's Venetian breakfast was a combination of al fresco and luncheon. Tables and chairs had been set up under an awning in the surprisingly large back garden, while blankets had been spread on the ground for the younger, more casual guests. Several faces were familiar to Gina, including Lord Calton, Lord and Lady Dominic Gorse, and Mrs. and Miss Dove. To Gina's relief, Lord Longton was not among the guests. To her disappointment, neither was Rollo.

The princess welcomed them as though genuinely pleased to see them, and offered them the tastiest morsels before turning to greet other guests. Gina, leaving Mrs. Fitzwilliam comfortably settled with her friends, took her plate and joined Catherine Dove and some of the younger people on a blanket.

After a while, as her companions changed positions or went to find more food, Gina and Miss Dove were private enough to risk a delicate conversation.

"May I ask you a strange question?" Gina began. "Well, two

strange questions, in strictest confidence?"

Catherine looked intrigued. "Please do."

"May I please borrow your dog tomorrow evening?"

Catherine stared at her, a delightfully prepared smoked fish halfway to her lips. She lowered it to her plate. "If you imagine Pup is a guard dog, I have to warn you he is not reliable. He looks threatening, but he is as likely to make friends with whoever it is you want to frighten."

"Oh, I don't want him to frighten anyone. I just want him to be obvious, and he is the most obvious dog I ever encountered."

Catherine ate her fish thoughtfully and swallowed. "You are up to something. May I join the adventure?"

"Sadly, no," Gina said with genuine regret, for the whole plan might have been fun with a friend. But this was not an expedition of pleasure. "It is not quite…proper, and you should not be seen with me."

Catherine looked even more curious but said only. "Pup is rarely away from us, and how would we get him to you?"

Gina had already thought of this. "Do you perhaps have a stable hand or a footman you can trust? To take Pup in a hackney and bring him home later on?"

"A hackney?" Catherine repeated, clearly startled. "Where are you taking him? I don't want him to get lost!"

Gina hesitated, glancing around her again. "Maida Gardens. Well, the hotel there, Renwick's. We are going to dine with my father there and spend the night before returning to town."

Catherine frowned. "It's most odd of you to want a huge, disruptive dog with you while you dine with your papa. And to be honest, we are not so rich in footmen or stable hands that one would not be missed, so I…" She trailed off, her frown vanishing. "Archie!"

Gina glanced over her shoulder, but there was no sign of Mr. Holles.

"If I asked him," Catherine pursued, "Archie would bring Pup to Renwick's for you and bring him home. And Pup will be happier in his company than with a servant."

Gina hesitated. "I am reluctant to involve him."

"Oh, he is the most discreet of men and totally honorable, I assure you."

"I never doubted that, just how unkind it would be to him."

"Now I am worried all over again! I believe, for your sake, I am making the loan of Pup dependent on Archie's bringing him. For your sake."

"Actually," Gina said slowly, "it might fit very well if he truly does not mind."

"I'll ask him, but he never refuses me. What is your other question?"

"Something I doubt you'll know, but I'm hoping you'll be able to point me to someone who does." Gina drew in a deep breath. "How and where would I find an actress willing to take discreet employment for one evening only?"

Catherine blinked several times. "Rollo Darblay."

Gina blushed. "I can't ask him this."

"Because he wouldn't let you do it?"

"I don't know," Gina said frankly, "but to involve him in this would not be...honorable."

"Besides, it would be difficult to ask a gentleman to introduce you to any actresses of their acquaintance. He would be appalled and embarrassed and very unlikely to help."

That many gentlemen had irregular relationships with actresses was not something Gina wished to dwell on, particularly where Rollo was concerned, but Catherine was gazing at their hostess.

"I have a better idea," she said. "I suspect you could do a lot worse than speak to Princess Hagerin. She may appear a mere fashionable hostess, but she has a mysterious past, and I know that she has helped several friends of mine in tricky situations. She is a friend of both the Duke and Duchess of Dearham, and I suspect she knows *everyone*."

"Thank you," Gina said gratefully, for she regarded this as the most difficult part of her plan to put in place. "And for the loan of Pup and your Mr. Holles."

While they made the arrangements, Gina kept a surreptitious watch on their hostess and chose her moment carefully. She waited until the princess was giving directions to servants, then rose and strolled toward her.

"What a lovely breakfast," Gina said. "I'm so glad I didn't eat before we came!"

Princess Hagerin looked faintly amused but behind the smile, her eyes were shrewd as ever and interested. She knew Gina had come to her for a reason. "The weather has been kind to us, too, though my cook insisted it would rain. Walk with me, Miss Wallace. You look like a lady with a confidence to make or break."

"Well, I do have a problem I am trying to solve," Gina admitted, turning to stroll with her hostess toward a little vegetable garden. "And I was wondering if you could help me with a rather difficult part of it."

"Does this problem involve Lord Longton?"

Gina's eyes flew to hers. "You are a friend of his lordship's?" she managed, for that could be disastrous, particularly if the princess told him Gina was up to something.

"No," Princess Hagerin said briefly. "Tell me how I might help you."

"I need to hire an actress for an evening, and I have no way of being introduced to such a person." She paused, wracking her brains for an un-insulting way of proceeding.

"To do what?" the princess asked as if this was a request she encountered every day from supposedly respectable young ladies.

"To pretend to win a great deal of money from me at cards. In company that might be considered questionable for a respectable, unmarried young lady."

"Or a respectable, betrothed young lady," the princess said. "Am I correct in imagining you do not wish to be betrothed?"

"Why would you think that?" Gina asked as lightly as she

could manage.

"I saw you with him at Lady Rampton's and at Mrs. Carrington's ball. Over the years, I have learned to read the signs. If you will believe such melodrama, my life has often depended on reading them correctly."

In which case, Gina devoutly hoped she had not read the signs when she was with Rollo. Or did she?

"Where do you want this actress to win money from you?" the princess asked.

"Renwick's Hotel."

"Maida Gardens." The princess regarded her thoughtfully. "When?"

"Tomorrow evening. From about nine o'clock."

The princess smiled. "Forget actresses. You will be much more discreet—and safe—losing lots of imaginary money to me. Tell me all."

Chapter Eleven

AT FIRST, FITZ was deeply annoyed by his aunt's assumption that he would trail out to Maida with her and Gina Wallace when he was supposed to be supporting James Black in a duel at dawn the following morning. But then, genius struck him, and he called round at Darblay House to discover Dom, Meade, and Montague already with the viscount.

"Had an idea," he said. "Why don't we go out to Renwick's the night before the duel?"

"Why is that a good idea?" Rollo demanded. He was seated at his desk, surrounded by a sea of crumpled pieces of paper, as if he had tried and failed many times to write an important letter.

"Have a bit of fun," Fitz said.

"Fun?" Dom stared at him. "He's going to fight a duel. Getting jug-bitten the night before, even against a novice swordsman, is hardly sensible."

"No, no, just meant a bit of dinner. And we'd all be in the right place with less trouble getting up early and trailing out to Maida."

"Shouldn't you be with Black?"

"We'll take him with us the night before. Who knows? He might even see sense and give the whole affair up once he gets to know us."

"He can't get to know me," Rollo pointed out. "We're not

supposed to speak directly until we've tried to kill each other."

"That's true," Montague said. "We'd have to travel separately. You two with Black, Meade and me with Rolls. But it's not such a bad idea to be there and fresh the next morning. Also gets us out of town and the curious wanting to know if it's true you're fighting a duel."

Rollo shrugged impatiently. "I don't much care. I just want it over. I have more important things to deal with. Shove off, now, there's good fellows. I'm busy."

Fitz, having achieved his aim without admitting his thrall to his aunt—or to Gina in an entirely different way—was happy enough to go. He and Dom decided to call on their own man to persuade him going to Renwick's the night before was a good idea.

"What's the matter with Rolls?" Dom said abruptly as they walked. "Is he sorting out his marriage at the same time as his duel?"

"I'm afraid it might be something like that," Fitz said ruefully. "But it won't be to the Smythe girl."

"No, I'm afraid it will be to Mrs. Snoddy. And it won't answer."

"No," Fitz said. "I don't suppose it will. But the poor fellow doesn't have many options, save borrowing from Wenning and his friends, and he's come over too proud."

"He always was," Dom said. "In his own way. All this raking about town was only ever a distraction to him. What he really wants is to run his own acres and be a simple country gentleman. Most of the time."

"Rollo?" Fitz said dubiously. "Are you sure?"

"Nope. But he does keep a fellow guessing. Come on, let's find our gudgeon and explain his pre-duel treat to him."

Despite all her anxieties—mostly involving her plan, her own willingness to deceive, and the fact that she had not seen or heard from Rollo—she found she was delighted to be reunited with her father. He was autocratic and so utterly determined on his family's social advancement, that he had not considered Gina's feelings. But he was her father, and she had missed him.

Mrs. Fitzwilliam, the eternally good-natured Fitz, Gina, and her father all dined privately in his sitting room at six o'clock, which was early by town standards. However, it was clear to Gina that her parent was tired from his long journey and needed an early night. Which suited her plans perfectly. However, she needed to know his.

"What brings you to town so soon, Papa?" she asked in a private moment. "We weren't expecting you until closer to the end of the month. Is everything well?"

"Oh, yes, of course, everything is fine. Your brother and sisters send their love. It just struck me Longton is playing us for fools."

"In what way?" Gina asked cautiously, trying not to be consumed by hope that he had changed his mind about her marriage. In which case, she would be able to cancel the elaborate charade.

"Laying down the law. Inspecting your performance in London society as though you're an ill-mannered horse. It's downright disrespectful, and so I shall tell him."

"You mean to break the engagement?" She had to fight not to sound delighted, or even hopeful.

He blinked. "Of course not. I gave my word. But it's time he gave his."

"You want to bring the wedding forward?" she asked faintly.

"Best thing for all of us. Can't be pleasant for you either, living with this uncertainty. But Mrs. Fitzwilliam tells me you have been quite taken in polite circles and that Longton is pleased with you. So, I've come to speak to him and set the date."

Gina sank onto the nearest sofa to deal with the abrupt loss of equally sudden hope and was very glad when the others joined them. Oh yes, she was right to have planned this evening, for her father would never, ever break his word, even, she suspected, if he knew it was wrong to keep it.

"You are tired, Papa," Gina said when they had consumed a very decent dinner. "Perhaps we should all retire early in order to make the most of tomorrow."

"I'll own several days in a bumping coach takes it out of me far more than rushing from mill to mill and office to office all day ever has," her father said.

Fitz's face perked, though he quickly covered the fact with a sympathetic expression.

"Well, we shall leave you for tonight, Papa, and meet again for breakfast," Gina proposed. "It was a lovely idea to meet us here."

"Very well-run, comfortable establishment," her father pronounced. "Though I am sorry to be such a dull companion."

Everyone assured him he was no such thing, and in spite of being still a tad indignant with him for his unkind disposal of her life, she kissed him goodnight with a rush of affection. She could not change him and did not wish to. But she had to look after herself, too.

Fitz conducted the ladies back to their suite of rooms—the same they had occupied the last time—and took himself off, no doubt in search of some congenial spirits with whom to enjoy a convivial evening.

Mrs. Fitzwilliam flopped down on the sofa. "It's rather an early end to the evening, is it not? Barely nine o'clock! We could play cards if you like."

Gina hesitated. She could not afford to spend hours playing cards with her chaperone. On the other hand, she didn't think Mrs. Fitz would believe her if she claimed exhaustion and retired at this time of the evening. Nor could she be sure Mrs. Fitz would retire when she did.

And Little would definitely be suspicious. On the other hand, she didn't really want to involve her kind chaperone in what was to follow, even if she had introduced Lord Longton to Papa. Perhaps, if things were still decorous, she would leave before long…

"Funnily enough, Princess Hagerin asked me the same thing! I had to decline because I assumed we would be with my father the whole evening. But she is holding a private card party here in the hotel."

"She is?" Mrs. Fitzwilliam looked astonished. "Why would she come all the way out here just to hold a card party?"

"I don't know," Gina replied brazenly. "Perhaps to accommodate friends from out of town. She has a very wide acquaintance, does she not?"

"That is very true. But she mentioned nothing to me, and I have received no card."

"I suppose she didn't bother to speak to you because I had already told her we were elsewhere engaged."

"She is quite easy-going," Mrs. Fitzwilliam reflected. "I'm sure she would not mind if we imposed for a little…" She frowned. "A very little. If the stakes are high, I cannot afford to play, Gina, and you *should* not."

"Oh, I'm sure it's just for fun," Gina lied, ignoring her conscience. When Mrs. Fitz saw the stakes were ridiculous, she would be more inclined to leave, and Gina would still have a chaperone in the princess.

Accordingly, they went in search of the princess's rooms and knocked on the door. It was opened by a liveried footman, whose fellow was offering trays of refreshments to the people within.

Princess Aline Hagerin, in magnificent evening dress, was standing in the middle of the sitting room, chatting to a couple of people, though most of the guests were seated, some already dealing cards. The majority were gentlemen, although a few elegant ladies graced the company, one middle-aged and two dashing young matrons.

And a very large dog, lying on the floor. He got up suddenly, wagging his tail and Archie Holles, who held the lead, gave Gina a sardonic smile.

The princess saw the newcomers at once and swept toward them. "You came! How delightful!"

"My father was tired after his journey, so we left him to sleep."

"Excellent, then we may play our promised challenge of piquet! Mrs. Fitzwilliam, a glass of wine? What would you like to play? Or would you prefer to sit and watch?"

Gina was in awe. Without the princess, she would have struggled to bring together such a mix of the respectable and the slightly ramshackle. She would certainly have struggled to place them so well, with the noisiest group of rakish young men close to her own piquet table and Archie Holles with Pup almost back-to-back with her. Though Archie held the lead, the dog lay half beside Gina so that she could stroke its great head and let it lick her hand occasionally.

In fact, as Gina commenced the serious business of losing to the princess, it struck her that the dog was behaving exceptionally well. According to Catherine, he got extremely excited in company.

She leaned back a little and spoke to Archie. "Thank you for doing this, sir."

"It's my pleasure, though I hope you know what you're about."

"So do I," she said fervently. "Is Pup quite well?"

"Thankfully, he seems to be overwhelmed. I don't believe he has ever been in company without at least one of his family present."

Since Mrs. Fitzwilliam was frowning at her from the sofa, Gina allowed herself to win the next hand with sensible play. Even so, her heart sank when her chaperone appeared at her side.

"My dear, these stakes are too high," she warned. "You should stop now."

"I have allowed myself so much, ma'am, and when my purse is empty, I will stop! Though my luck is clearly turning. Will you not play?"

"No, I believe I will seek my bed. Princess, might I rely on you to take care of my young friend?"

Gina breathed a sigh of relief. At least Mrs. Fitz was not provoking a quarrel to make her leave at the same time. The stage was almost set...

"I shall act as the strictest chaperone in your absence, Mrs. Fitzwilliam," the princess said kindly. "If you are determined to leave us, let me show you out. Be assured I shall return her right to the door of your rooms. Excuse me one moment, Miss Wallace."

Gina watched the quiet conversation as the two women walked to the door. Mrs. Fitzwilliam gave a relieved smile. Then the footman opened the door and she was gone. The princess rustled back to her chair.

"What did you say to her?" Gina murmured.

"Not to worry. That I would not take your winnings but was merely showing you how quickly one could be ruined playing for such high stakes."

"The aim being to sicken me of gambling before I marry?"

The princess smiled brilliantly. "Another hand?"

"If we raise the stakes..."

Everything was going exactly to plan, now. In front of the princess was piled all the money Gina had with her, including several large notes weighed down with coins. She had just written out her first promissory vowel when the unthinkable happened.

A peremptory knock on the door had Gina's heart beating fast with anticipation. She and the princess exchanged breathless glances.

The footman opened the door—to reveal *not* Lord Longton but several young men.

The footman glanced back at the princess for instruction. She rose to her feet as one gentleman pushed to the front.

"Evening, Aline," Rollo Darblay said cheerfully. "May we be so rude as to—" He broke off, his eyes widening as they clashed with Gina's.

And then the dog erupted with joy.

◆

Rollo was utterly thrown by her presence. Had she somehow got wind of the stupid duel? Had some idiot found his letter to her and given it to her without him actually dying? Or did she know about…?

Confusion crystalized into entirely unreasonable fury as the quality of her companions struck him. A few fast women, and a collection of drunken rakehells with whom he was well acquainted.

The cry of his name went up from the latter. "Rolls!" At the same time, about half a ton of dog hit him like a cannonball. Meade and Dom held him upright while a large tongue slathered over his face.

"Catch him, Darblay!" came the unlikely voice of Archie Holles—he was far too serious to be among this lot of wastrels.

Rollo gazed into adoring canine eyes. "Pup?"

None of this made sense. But at least some instinct made him grab the beast's collar as he hauled him off and then pick up the leash, which had clearly been yanked out of someone's hand.

"My new dog," Archie said, hurrying to take the leash from him. "The princess was kind enough to let him stay, but he—"

"His lordship is quite unhurt," the princess interrupted. "And at least the beast didn't knock over any furniture. My lords, gentlemen, welcome. I imagine you need no introduction to my other guests. A glass of wine?" The footman came forward with the tray. "Please, be seated where you will, or just watch the play."

Rollo barely managed a bow before he made a beeline straight for Gina. Her eyes were trying to convey something to him, but he was far too angry to decipher it. All he saw was desperation, pleading, a hint of shame.

"Miss Wallace." He bowed, almost as if throwing the courtesy at her. "May I?"

"Sadly not, my lord. The princess and I are in the midst of play."

Stupidly, the refusal made him even angrier, and then he saw the mountain of money and vowels sitting by the princess's seat. He lowered his voice. "Where is Mrs. Fitzwilliam?"

"In bed, I imagine," said Princess Aline. "If you please, my lord?"

Impatiently, he shifted and held the princess's chair for her, though he immediately stepped closer to Gina. "For God's sake, let me take you to her."

"That would not be proper, my lord. Princess, your card."

Dismissed, Rollo felt the world getting away from him all over again. Gina had somehow righted it, given him an anchor, a strategy. Given him *hope* along with need. And so much more. And yet there she sat, just like *him*, damn her, up to her neck in debt in dubious company he knew all too well.

A half-empty glass of red wine even sat by her elbow. A drop had spilled on the otherwise pristine white lace of her elegant evening gown and another on the glove beside her. Rage, not so much with her as at whatever or whoever had put her in such a position, all but overwhelmed him. Then someone had an arm through his—Dom—and pulled him away toward a game of hazard.

The stakes were high, and fortunately, perhaps, no chairs were available. Rollo, after glowering unseeingly at the game for a few moments, dragged Fitz back from it.

"You have to take her back to your aunt."

"How do you propose I do that without raising a storm?" demanded Fitz, who had been skulking behind the others for some reason since they had come in.

"Is she even here at Renwick's?"

"Of course she is," Fitz said indignantly. "Brought them both myself. Had dinner with *Mr.* Wallace."

Rollo glared at him. "And you never thought to say?" *Gina* had never thought to say, and that hurt more badly than anything. Of course, he had not been near her for the last few days, for fear he would give away the annoyance of his forthcoming duel, so he had hardly given her opportunity. But he had missed her abominably.

"None of your business, Rolls," Fitz pointed out, and Rollo clenched his hands.

Gina stood up, and Rollo watched her retreat into what was probably the princess's bedchamber. He could hardly disturb her there, but he moved around the other tables, determined to accost her when she came out again.

"Don't," murmured a feminine voice in his ear, and he turned to find Aline Hagerin pressing another glass of wine into his hand. He hadn't touched the last one. "You'll draw attention to her and that's the last thing she needs. Ignore her."

As it seemed she would ignore him. She emerged from the bedchamber and slipped around the tables farthest away from him to resume her seat. The princess rustled away from Rollo to join her.

It didn't help his mood that the princess was correct. Her position in such a gathering was precarious at best. To be singled out by a notorious rakehell in the company would most definitely intensify the gossip to the edge of ruin.

But he was damned if he would leave her. Catching sight of the dog once more, he frowned and slouched over to join Holles, throwing himself into the conveniently vacant chair beside him, from where he could see both Gina and the play at her table.

At Holles's table, play was just finishing up and discussion ensuing as to whether or not to change the game.

"That's not your dog, Holles," Rollo murmured. "It's the Doves' monster or I'm a lemon."

"For tonight he's mine."

"Why?"

"Damned if I know," Holles admitted. "Catherine asked it of me."

Rollo met his gaze. "They're up to something," he breathed. "And the truly damnable thing is, we can't help in any way because we don't know what would make it worse." *If anything could.*

It certainly got worse. While apparently drinking affably with Holles, Rollo was appalled to see Gina lose and lose more to the princess. She laughed it off with all the carelessness of a very wealthy young woman. Rollo did not doubt that she could afford to lose it, but he could not understand Princess Aline continuing to play with her.

Although on first-name terms with her, he did not know the princess well. But several of his friends, including Johnny Dearham and Harry de Vere, thought very highly of her. In fact, gossip once said that Dearham would marry her, back in the days when he was merely heir to the dukedom. Rumor also said that during the late wars, she had done the British government many favors at great personal risk. Why would such a woman fleece a vulnerable innocent like Gina?

As for Gina herself...was this merely another aspect of the recklessness that had thrown her into his arms in this very hotel? He could not understand or even separate the turbulent emotions tearing him apart.

Gina was writing out yet another vowel. The footman opened the door and bowed before admitting the unmistakable figure of Mrs. Snodgrass.

And behind her, none other than Lord Longton.

Blood sang in Rollo's ears. He began to get an inkling of what Gina was about. *"He has quite definite ideas of what he doesn't want in a wife. I just have to convince him I have those foibles in spades."*

Aline rose, and the newcomers' attention went straight to her and then to Gina, just as a promissory vowel on a scrap of paper floated from her elegant fingers to land on the large pile in front of her opponent.

Rollo tensed. He would not allow her to be insulted by anyone, least of all by that hypocritical old windbag who had once been a close friend of his father's.

CHAPTER TWELVE

*A*T LAST.
Gina had sent Mrs. Snodgrass a long letter yesterday, to which she had replied only that she would do her best. And she had, for Longton was right behind her.

The moment was now, and Gina could barely breathe. And yet through it all was her misery that Rollo was angry with her, that in her attempt to be rid of Longton and save her father's pride, she had ruined her nascent love before it had a chance. That it would all be for nothing.

His eyes bored into the side of her face as she gazed amiably across the room at the newcomers. She nodded civilly to Mrs. Snodgrass and smiled at Lord Longton.

The princess rose to greet her new guests, and Gina let her hand fall to Pup's enormous head. Obligingly, he rubbed his face against her hand, giving her the excuse to make a big fuss of him. She even fed him a morsel from the princess's plate. Then she rose and strolled toward the door.

Longton's gaze was on the table and the heap of vowels and money at the princess's side. On Gina's abandoned gloves, on the dog.

"Mrs. Snodgrass, how do you do?" she said, offering her hand, which the lady shook with perfect courtesy. "My lord."

Longton shrank back, staring with horror as her hand slipped from Mrs. Snodgrass's hold. Presumably, he feared she would also offer it to him after she had been petting the dog. Well, she would not invite insult.

"I'm sorry I can't stay, now that you have arrived," she said gaily, "but I am quite rolled up for the next two quarters and must seek my bed before Mrs. Fitzwilliam scolds me. Princess Aline had all the luck. But I thank you for the vastly entertaining evening, ma'am!"

"Then I shall accompany you along the passage to your rooms as I promised your chaperone," the princess said before turning back to Longton and Mrs. Snodgrass with a quick smile. "Please, make yourselves at home, and I shall return in one minute. Dennis, some wine here, if you please," she added to the hovering footman.

"Please don't trouble," Longton said disdainfully. "I shall not be staying."

"No?" The princess sounded disappointed. "But several of your particular friends are here! See, there is Sir Mortimer, and Mrs. Cannon is waving to you."

That, Gina thought in awe, *was a beautiful touch.* But if Longton noticed his hypocrisy being pointed out, he gave no sign of it, merely bowing to his acquaintances and holding the door for the ladies to precede him.

Gina sailed through and would have kept walking, except that Longton spoke sharply behind her as soon as the door was closed.

"A moment with Miss Wallace, if you please, Princess."

"I'm not sure I can allow that, standing in as I do, for Mrs. Fitzwilliam," Aline replied.

"It's fine," Gina said without turning. "Mrs. Fitz knows that his lordship and I are old friends." She heard the sound of his footsteps stalking up to her.

"Is this sort of behavior condoned by your father?" he snapped.

Gina feigned surprise and crossed her fingers behind her back. "I don't know, but you could ask him. He has rooms next to ours."

Longton's eyes narrowed. "How much have you lost this evening, madam?"

"That is not yet any of your business, my lord."

"It will never be any of my business. You are a disgrace. You reek of dog, and there is wine all over your clothing."

"There will be wine all over yours if you are brave enough to insult me so in front of a true gentleman."

A purple tinge had crept into his complexion. "Consider all agreements between us at an end."

"Be so good as to write to my father to that effect before you leave the hotel. Since I was never party to the agreement, it is clearly nothing to do with me. Goodnight, my lord."

As she spun away from him, she suddenly found Rollo at one side of her.

"Your gloves, Miss Wallace. Allow me to escort you and the princess to your door."

She inclined her head, hoping he could not see the shaking of her entire body. The princess stood on her other side, while Mrs. Snodgrass took Longton's arm in a soothing grip. At the same time, she secretly found Gina's hand and squeezed it. Gratefully, Gina squeezed back and went on her trembling way.

"You did it," the princess whispered with something very like unholy glee.

"No, ma'am," Gina said huskily. "You and Mrs. Snodgrass did it. With a little help from Pup and Mr. Holles. And Catherine."

"But not me," Rollo said grimly.

He was still angry. *Oh, please, God, please don't let him stay angry with me...*

"Why on earth would we involve you, Rollo?" the princess drawled. "You are in mourning, with more than enough on your plate from what I hear."

Rollo cast her a quick, almost questioning look, but at least he did not berate her. And then they were at the door of the rooms she shared with Mrs. Fitzwilliam.

"Goodnight, my lord," the princess said firmly.

"I, too, need a private word with Miss Wallace," Rollo said.

"Not now, my lord," Gina said firmly, though she offered him her hand, and when their eyes met, she tried to will him to understand. She had no idea if he did though, as she freed her hand and hugged Princess Aline. "Thank you. Thank you for everything."

And then she slipped inside the door and closed it.

A single lamp burned dimly in the sitting room.

"Is that you, Gina?" came Mrs. Fitzwilliam's voice, muffled from her bedchamber door.

"Yes, the princess accompanied me back. Goodnight, Mrs. Fitz."

"Goodnight."

As she crossed toward her own chamber, dropping her stained gloves and reticule on the table, Little appeared at the door of the maids' room.

"Go to bed, Little," Gina said calmly. "I shan't need you until the morning. I can manage the hooks on this gown quite easily."

"But I—"

"Good night, Little."

The maid swallowed and retreated, closing the door with a snap.

Gina whisked into her own room, snatched the traveling cloak from its place behind the door, and swung it around her shoulders before creeping back out, across the sitting room, and out into the corridor.

He hadn't understood. He hadn't waited. The disappointment was like a blow, the need to see him, touch him, explain, like a physical pain.

A shadow moved at the corner of the passage and resolved into the figure of a man.

"It's me."

Relief flooded her. She ran toward the figure, but he did not crush her in his arms as she expected. Instead, he snatched her hand and bolted through a door onto a well-lit back stairway. They ran up the steps together to another quiet passage, and Rollo opened the nearest door with a key. Pulling her inside, he closed and locked it again and turned up the lamp.

Words fell over each other in her need to make him understand everything, yet all that came out was, "Rollo, I—" before his arms came hard around her and his mouth seized hers.

With a sob, she threw her arms around his neck and pulled him closer, kissing him back with all the passion she had learned from him.

"I know," he muttered between kisses. "You got rid of him, made *him* break the agreement so your father didn't have to."

"He hates gambling in women, slovenly women, scandalous women, pert women, dogs…"

Rollo's mouth smiled against hers. "Arch hypocrite."

She drew back slightly, taking his head between her hands so that she could look into his face. "I was afraid you felt the same. You looked at me with such anger."

"Oh, not for you, never for you. I was afraid I had driven you to dissipation, made you like *me,* and for that, I'd never forgive myself. And I confess I was furious not to be included in your plans, not even to know of them. I was hurt, like some sulky schoolboy."

She smiled tenderly, tracing his lips with her fingers. "I love this sulky schoolboy."

"Oh, thank God." His arms tightened convulsively. "I don't know how you can, but I'll take it with gratitude and joy. Will you marry me?"

"Oh yes," she breathed, fusing her mouth to his.

"And that was the other part of your plan," Rollo said, some moments later, throwing her cloak on the floor and starting on the hooks of her gown. "To have an alternative title on hand as a sop to your father's pride."

"To marry you was the *original* plan. Beyond any plans, it became my need. *Rollo!*" The last was a gasp, not of outrage but of sheer, unbearable pleasure as he attached his mouth to her nipple.

Still kissing her, he lifted her in his arms and deposited her on the bed, his hands sweeping everywhere in knowing, sensual caresses, even while they removed every item of her clothing and she wrenched at his. And then she let out a sob of joy as he pushed inside her, making them one again at last.

He groaned softly, closing his eyes for a moment before they blazed down at her with predatory intent. "I, too, have been busy," he said huskily, beginning to move above her, in her. Bliss took her by surprise, shaking her to her core, but he barely paused, giving her no time to gather herself, only to wallow and arch and moan. "Among other things, I acquired a special license. We can be married tomorrow if we can find a clergyman to do it."

"Oh God, I love you," she whispered, clinging to him, moving with him toward an inexorable, mutual, cataclysmic pleasure.

"And I love you," he breathed into her open mouth as he collapsed upon her. "Only you. Forever and ever and ever."

GINA WOKE WITH languorous contentment. She had fallen asleep in Rollo's arms, unable to make herself leave him just yet, even though she told herself she should. *Just five more minutes*, she had promised herself, for after the intoxicating physical love, had come sheer, uncomplicated happiness, a sense of rightness that here in his arms was exactly where she was meant to be.

And here she still was, although there was movement in the passage outside the door. She stretched out her arm, but Rollo was not there. For a moment, a sense of abandonment hurt her. But only for a moment.

Rollo loved her. Rollo had a special license in his pocket to marry her. He had probably gone to order coffee or breakfast or to ask Aline to cover for her absence with Mrs. Fitzwilliam.

Only, it was still dark.

She sat up and lit the lamp by the bed. Then she rose, found Rollo's washing water and tooth powder, and made use of both, before slipping back into her chemise and gown and cloak. Under the cloak, she hid her stays, which were too difficult to lace up by herself.

The movement and voices from the passage seemed to have stopped. Perhaps some late revelers heading finally to bed. She opened the door a crack, and finding the corridor empty, she pulled up her hood, slid out of the room, and closed the door behind her.

Unseen, she flitted along the passage to the stairs, and then along the quiet passage to her own rooms. Using her key, she crept into silence and darkness. She made it unseen to her own room and undressed to her chemise.

She was reaching for her night rail when from outside this time, more muffled voices reached her, along with a rumble of quiet laughter and soft footsteps. She padded to the window and drew back the curtain.

A scattering of mostly silent men were making their way away from the hotel and along the path to the fields beyond.

What on earth…?

It came to her that Rollo was probably with them since he wasn't in his bed. She further realized that she had no idea why he had come to Renwick's. He had been surprised to see her, so he hadn't come for her. And with her knowledge of him, her trust in him, she knew he had not brought some ladybird here. She was certain the princess had not invited him, but he had chosen to come anyway, along with his friends—Mr. Meade and Mr. Montague, Lord Dominic Gorse and…had that been Fitz skulking behind them?

Godfrey Fitzwilliam's presence struck her fully for the first time. Why would Fitz have avoided Gina at the card party?

Something suspicious was going on.

Instead of her night rail, Gina donned her new lavender walking dress and matching hat, swung the cloak back around her shoulders, and sallied forth. Just in time to see Fitz creeping from his room on the other side of the passage.

At sight of her, he froze. Then, recovering, he said, "It's too early to be up and about. Not quite dawn you know."

"You are up and about," she pointed out.

"Couldn't sleep. Going for a walk."

"Along with all the other men in the hotel?"

"What?" He looked genuinely confused.

"Is there a prizefight? A cock fight or something?"

"I expect it's something like that," Fitz said with a hint of relief. "I'll just go and find out and let you know."

"I'll come with you."

"You can't do that! Not the thing for a lady. You wouldn't like it."

"Well, once I find out what it is, I can leave again, curiosity satisfied."

"Dash it, you can't be seen with me at this time of the morning!" Fitz exclaimed. "People will talk, and Aunt will draw and quarter me."

Another figure loomed around the corner. "Fitz? Time to go."

It was Lord Dominic Gorse, and at his side, a young man Gina had never seen before.

"Miss Wallace?" Dominic said cautiously.

"Fitz has been refusing to take me to your prizefight."

"Quite right, too," Lord Dominic agreed.

"Then it *is* a prizefight? Fitz didn't seem very sure."

"It's not a prizefight," Princess Aline's voice said softly. "I've been up there, and there's no fighting ring, just a lot of young men making wagers and a fiddler."

"A fiddler?" Lord Dominic said with a sudden grin. "Come on, fellows, let's go. We're desolate, ladies, not to have your company. Good morning."

Gina and Aline watched them vanish down the staircase.

Then it struck Gina like a blow. "It's not a prizefight, it's a duel…"

"I suspect so."

"But who…?"

"I suspect the young man we don't know and Lord Darblay."

Gina's mouth fell open. "Rollo? But why?"

"A very silly, vain girl—one Miss Smythe—has been spreading rumors that Lord Darblay compromised her and won't marry her. Some banker's son took it upon himself to challenge Rollo."

"But that's nonsense!" Gina was already marching for the staircase.

"I came along to be sure you knew nothing," Aline said, "and were safely tucked up in bed. But it seems events are now beyond me."

"Well, they're not beyond me," Gina said grimly.

Aline caught her hand. "Gina. You can't interfere without ruining your own name."

"It doesn't matter. I won't have Rollo killed for a stupid lie!"

"Gina, he won't be killed," the princess said bluntly. "He's fought before, you know."

"And if he kills the other man?"

"That is more of a problem, but—"

Gina sailed on, and after a moment, Aline merely walked beside her, casting her odd glances that might have held admiration.

They had almost caught up with Fitz and his companions by the time they reached the male gathering in the meadow. The first light of dawn was beginning to break, revealing a few young men sitting in trees, others sprawled on blankets and folding chairs in the grass. They were all cheering as Rollo, facing them, swore at them and told them to go home.

And then the fiddler started up and he let out one of his familiar cracks of laughter. "Oh, for the love of—"

"It's a damned circus," exclaimed the banker's son, who had

stopped in front of Gina to glare in outrage at the proceedings.

"You're quite within your rights to walk away," Lord Dominic told him. "This is not how an affair of honor should be conducted."

"Happy to make that point to Darblay's seconds," Fitz said. "You should just walk away."

Gina said, "If I might have a word with Mr....?"

"Black," Lord Dominic said with a sigh. "Mr. James Black. Black, this is Princess Aline Hagerin and Miss Wallace."

Black glanced at them impatiently, managed a jerky bow, and then froze. "Wait a moment. Miss *Wallace*? Then you were there when Lord Darblay assaulted Miss...that is, the young lady!"

"Yes, I was there," Gina said sternly, "and the only person assaulted was *me*. In point of fact, I was with his lordship when the young lady hurled herself into me, all but knocking me over in order to clutch his lordship and cry ruination. Mr. Meade and Mr. Montague had to drag her off him. They were meant to witness events, of course, only they were a few seconds too early for her purposes."

In the pale light, Mr. Black seemed to whiten. "Meade and Montague told me some such nonsense. But they did not mention you."

"Well, they wouldn't, would they?" the princess said gently. "Being gentlemen. The truth is, Mr. Black, that your good nature, your honor, and your trust have been manipulated by an unscrupulous young woman who is quite unworthy of your regard, let alone your life. And Darblay has done nothing to dishonor anyone."

"Except Miss Wallace, by the sound of it!" Black said in clearly a last-ditch attempt to find motive for his challenge.

"I was not assaulted by Lord Darblay. On the contrary, although I will be obliged by your discretion on this point for a few days, I am engaged to marry his lordship. Now please, let that be an end to this foolishness."

"Foolishness it is," Mr. Meade said cheerfully as he and Montague joined them. "Ladies, not sure you should be here, but not sure anything should happen anyway. What do you think, Dom?"

"I think Black might be ready to reconsider."

Mr. Black was pulling at his lower lip, irresolute, and no doubt reluctant to be thought a coward by backing down.

"Perhaps," Lord Dominic suggested, "we should convey apologies to Lord Darblay for your misunderstanding of the situation at the ball? Tell him that in the light of new information, you are happy to accept his version of events?"

"That would work," Mr. Montague said. "Shall I speak to Rolls?"

Mr. Black hesitated one moment more, then nodded. Meade and Montague grinned and sauntered back to Rollo, who was still exchanging amiable insults with his audience to the accompaniment of jolly fiddle music.

"I believe our work here is done," Aline murmured as Lord Dominic led his principal toward Rollo's group.

"I believe it is," Gina agreed, but still she lingered to be sure. Then, suddenly, she frowned. "How did Mr. Black know my name?"

"None of the seconds would have mentioned you, and Darblay certainly wouldn't have. My money is on Miss Smythe herself when she convinced poor Black of the wrong done to her. I suspect her few invitations into polite society have dried up."

"Will mine?" Gina asked bluntly.

"No, my dear. Even last night, you were every inch a lady."

Not when I was in Rollo's bed. Again...

"Oh, no, Rolls, unfair!" came a shout from the tree branch. "We were lured here for the promise of a fencing match! You won't wriggle out of it! Got a damned monkey on you for first blood!"

"Tough," Rollo answered, picking up one of the rapiers from an open case at his feet and testing its point. He paused, and Gina could feel his speculation even over the distance between them. He was smiling as he spoke to Black. And even Black raised a reluctant laugh. So did the fiddle.

"Fencing tournament!" cried Rollo, throwing off his coat. "Buttons on foils, first touch—no blood!"

IT WAS AN hour later before Gina returned to the hotel with Princess Aline and a trail of loud, happy gentlemen, led by Rollo and Mr. Black, arm-in-arm. Most of those present had tried their hand with one of the two sets of matched rapiers present, the betting had flowed, and the audience had been treated to a display of sword skills. Gina, who had witnessed nothing like it before, was entranced and had drawn nearer until Rollo caught sight of her and almost dropped his weapon.

When she had smiled, he grinned back and fought on. In fact, she was impressed by his unexpected skill, aroused by the play of muscle in his arms and chest, and the speed of his almost-dancing feet. Familiar heat pooled low in her belly.

Through it all, the fiddler had played his merry tunes and received a fortune in tips along, presumably, with his original fee.

Entirely happy with the world, she entered the hotel, only to come face to face with her father and Mrs. Fitzwilliam.

The smile faded from her lips, for she could see at once that Papa had received Lord Longton's promised letter.

"Good morning, ma'am. Papa," she said civilly. "Are we having breakfast downstairs?"

"Assuredly not," barked her father, glaring at the throngs of noisy young men now pouring into the hotel behind Rollo and Mr. Black. As she parted from Aline with a smile and moved toward the staircase, far more calmly than she felt, she heard calls for Rollo to join his friends.

She didn't hear his reply.

Inevitably, Papa loosed his fury as soon as the door of their sitting room closed. "What have you done to alienate Lord

Longton?" he all but bellowed.

"Very little. But then, I did nothing to attract him either. You dangled money, and he leapt for it. No one troubled to consult me."

Papa glowered. "I have every right! Do you deny it?"

"No. But I am of age, Papa, and entitled to say yay or nay. To save your name, I persuaded Longton to do the nay-saying."

The wind seemed to leave her father's sails abruptly, and he sank onto the sofa looking like an old man. "Why?" he asked bewildered. "You agreed at the time. Longton's an earl. He would have given you a title, standing, made the way easier for your sisters and your brother…"

"I don't love him," Gina said frankly. "And don't dare tell me love does not count, for you loved Mama with a passion. All I wanted was the same right, the same privilege to choose. Admittedly, I should have discovered this earlier, and well before I left for London and met…"

"Met who?" her father asked with ominous quiet.

"Another titled lord whom I *do* intend to marry."

"Over my dead body!"

"I hope not, even without your blessing."

A brisk knock sounded at the door, and with hope, Gina started toward the door.

"Leave it!" her father snapped.

"Forgive me, Papa, but I want you to meet someone now." She knew before she opened the door that it would be Rollo, but she still couldn't help her smile to see him there. He wore a clean shirt and cravat, and his hair and coat had been well brushed. He bowed with a quick upward flick of one eyebrow, and she held out her hand to him. When he took it, she drew him into the room.

Her father rose, hands clenched hard at his side.

"Allow me to present my father, Mr. Robert Wallace," she said. "Papa, this is Viscount Darblay."

Rollo bowed with perfect propriety. "Very pleased to meet

you, at last, sir."

"You were one of those clowns fencing up in the meadow," Papa accused.

"I was," Rollo admitted. "You could call me the chief clown. Perhaps not the best introduction, since I've come to ask for your blessing. I want to marry your daughter."

"Rakes and fortune hunters need not apply for my daughter's hand!"

"I'm not applying to you for her hand," Rollo said before Gina could open her mouth. "She has already granted me permission and agreed to be my wife. I'm no catch, sir," he added as Papa was about to interrupt with fury. "I know that. My past is littered with scandal and mistakes, and my finances are a mess. But my family is an old one, and I will make her a viscountess. Even without your blessing or a penny of your money, I will make her a viscountess and count myself the most fortunate of men. But your blessing matters to her a great deal. She has moved heaven and earth to do this in such a way that leaves your word and your dreams intact. My hope is that you will do as much for her."

Mrs. Fitzwilliam sniffed into her handkerchief. Gina regarded her betrothed with considerable awe. Her hand crept into his as she turned to face her father.

"Please, Papa."

There was silence. Then; "Viscount, eh? Not as good as an earl."

"My sister is married to an earl," Rollo offered. "And if you like, I can bore you rigid with all the plans I would like to put in place to make my estates profitable again."

"With my Gina's money," Papa growled.

"With or without," Rollo replied steadily. "It will take longer without, but I *will* do it."

Papa took a step closer, and Gina's fingers tightened on Rollo's as she prepared to leap between the men. But Papa only stared into Rollo's eyes. He was *looking*, as he would at a prospective business partner of any kind. As he had failed to do with Longton, too dazzled by the title to see the man.

Her father gave a crooked smile. "I believe you will," he said unexpectedly. "Have breakfast, and I'll decide whether or not you are worthy."

"Happy to," Rollo said.

By the time they had had breakfast, strolled around the pleasure garden, and listened to the midday concert, Papa was conversing easily with Rollo and laughing at his jokes. By the time they reached the town, he had given his gracious permission to marry. And by the time Rollo had told him about the special license, he was so flabbergasted that he said not a word when Rollo kissed Gina a very long and affectionate goodbye until the morrow.

And when the wedding was performed in Mrs. Fitzwilliam's drawing room the following afternoon, he was beaming.

Gina, holding tight to her husband's hand, accepted with pleasure all the felicitations of Rollo's family, from his tearful mother to his smiling sisters and the urbane Lord Wenning.

And then at last they were alone, and he reminded her exactly why she was so happy to be his wife. He was her one and only gentleman of pleasure.

About Mary Lancaster

Mary Lancaster lives in Scotland with her husband, three mostly grown-up kids and a small, crazy dog.

Her first literary love was historical fiction, a genre which she relishes mixing up with romance and adventure in her own writing. Her most recent books are light, fun Regency romances written for Dragonblade Publishing: *The Imperial Season* series set at the Congress of Vienna; and the popular *Blackhaven Brides* series, which is set in a fashionable English spa town frequented by the great and the bad of Regency society.

Connect with Mary on-line – she loves to hear from readers:

Email Mary:
Mary@MaryLancaster.com

Website:
www.MaryLancaster.com

Newsletter sign-up:
http://eepurl.com/b4Xoif

Facebook:
facebook.com/mary.lancaster.1656

Facebook Author Page:
facebook.com/MaryLancasterNovelist

Twitter:
@MaryLancNovels

Amazon Author Page:
amazon.com/Mary-Lancaster/e/B00DJ5IACI

Bookbub:
bookbub.com/profile/mary-lancaster

CPSIA information can be obtained
at www.ICGtesting.com
Printed in the USA
BVHW091846060522
636356BV00015B/592